Fifty Grades of Shaved

Written by Nick Morley

Cover illustration by The Ghost.

WARNING This book contains explicit gay sexual content.

This book is dedicated to everyone who
has helped with the formation of it.

It is also dedicated to all my good friends
who gave their feedback on the stories before
publication. You know who you are. Thank you!

Special thanks to 'The Ghost' for the cover design.

Back to basics

Sometimes it's good to look back. To see the changes you have made and the achievements in your life. However, you can also unlock things that you buried for a reason. But sometimes, it's just plain necessary.

Friday

5.50. Just ten more minutes and I can go home. I can not wait. The novelty of working in this small office in London ...just me, three women and my manager Mr. Jefferson (who takes customer relations advice from Hitler), has well and truly worn off. It's Friday night! In 10 minutes I can finish in this hell hole for the weekend, get chips on the way home and crash out. Heaven!

5.55. And the excitement is beginning to build. I am doing nothing on my computer, I just have a word document up and making out I am working. But if he ever got off his backside and saw what I was really doing, I would be fired here and now. At that moment, the tyrant raises his head.

"Oh, Nick… I forgot to mention. Mandy is off work tomorrow and the Creston account needs to be sorted by Monday. You will have to stay behind to get it done."

"But Mr. Jefferson, I leave in 5 minutes. I have plans tonight!"

"You? You have plans?"

"Yes. I'm meeting my parents and we are going out for a meal."

What a lie. It was well known I had no plans... I never had any plans. I have never been any good at lying.

"Well the quicker you get it done; the quicker you will be able to eat! Get the file from the cabinet. If you need to call your parents I will allow you to use the company phone….this once."

I sighed and walked over to the filing cabinet. 6 o'clock. The girls stood up and put on their coats. I don't know if they were embarrassed to say goodbye as I had to stay or just didn't care. But they all filed out of the office without saying a word. Mr. Jefferson began to do his nightly ritual of making sure all lids were on his pens, clearing his desk and locking his drawers.

He was a real weasel of a man. He had short dark hair, gelled heavily and a face that only a mother could love.... and plenty would want to slap. He was short, bolshy and lived and died in a suit that he had bought for a family wedding and wanted to get the maximum use out of.

"Close the windows and the blinds when you leave. Oh, and put the alarm on …7256"

"Yes, Mr. Jefferson," I replied, like a Stepford husband.

As the office door closed, I breathed a huge sigh, half of despair at having to stay and half of relief that he had gone. First things first, if I'm staying, I'm getting something out of this. I picked up the phone and called for a pizza. True, it would stink the office out but that would have gone by Monday.

***

It was 9.30 when I finally managed to leave. I locked the office and began to walk down the road toward my flat. My route home took me past a pub which had always had a dubious reputation. It was a gay skinhead pub and I had been warned on many occasions to avoid it like the plague. My normal leaving time meant there was usually never anyone around outside. And if there was, there was always someone close that could help me if I got into any trouble. But this was not my normal time!

As I turned the corner the pub was on my right. I started walking towards it when I saw this bloke. He was chatting to some mates with his back to the road. As I went passed he turned round and looked at me. He said nothing but I nearly shit myself. He was a little taller than me, aggressive looking, with smooth shaved head, a checked shirt and bleachers, underneath a thick black coat. Our eyes locked as I passed and I could feel something stirring inside me. Once I had passed, I looked back to see him still staring at me.

"Pitch. Pitch! Come on mate, it's getting cold out here."

I watched as he stubbed his cigarette out on the wall and dropped it on the floor before disappearing inside.

I know what I should have done. I should have gone home. I should have just gone home and everything would have been OK. But I couldn't. There was something about that pub that had awoken my curiosity. That man, that intimidating image was burned into my brain and I had to see him again. Don't get me wrong, I may be a bit of a wet blanket but I'm not stupid. I know that if I hadn't have been walking past at that specific time, he wouldn't have looked twice at me. In fact, if I could pluck up the courage to go into that place...he still probably wouldn't. But that's not what happened. I took a deep breath and found myself opening the door.

***

The warmth and smell of sweat in the pub struck me as soon as I entered. What was I doing? What the hell was I doing? I walked over to the bar.

"What can I get you mate?" the barman asked.

"Erm…" I knew I couldn't ask for lemonade... I would have been laughed out of the pub. "Lager please," I finally piped up.

Once I had paid, I stood against a wall and looked around. I felt (and looked) like a fish out of water. I couldn't have stuck out any more if I had been dressed as a bloody clown. Everyone was staring… I felt so self-conscious. Then I saw him… Pitch. He was standing with his mates who were engrossed in conversation. He didn't even see me. He must have been the only one that didn't.

"Alright mate? Are you sure you're in the right place?" a voice asked.

As I turned around, I saw a very handsome man standing before me. He had a white polo shirt on, under a green flight jacket and tight bleachers were tucked into his large boots, which hugged his legs. He had large stars tattooed on the inside of both of his ears with dots running down to multiple studs, a cross under his left eye and a swallow on his right scalp with JS behind his right ear.

"I'm beginning to wonder," I smiled, feeling something begin to stir in my pants.

"My name's John!"

"Nick."

"If you don't mind me saying, you don't look very comfortable."

"Is it that obvious?"

"Just a little," he laughed.

My eyes flicked back to the guy outside who was still talking, oblivious to my presence.

"Oh mate, you have got good taste. That's not a man….that is a God!"

"What? I ….no, I was just passing and thought I would have a drink."

"Mate, no one ever just passes here!"

"I saw him outside. Do you know him?"

"No. But I would fucking like to! Everyone calls him Pitch."

"Pitch?" I asked, making sure I had heard him correctly.

"Yeah. It's short for picture because of all the tattoos he has."

"What's his real name?"

"I don't know. He has been called Pitch for so long, I don't think he would answer to his real name." John paused, thinking if he should say something. "Can I be honest?"

"Sure," I replied, praying he wouldn't.

"If you go over there and talk to him, one of two things is going to happen. One, he will just ignore and belittle you….or two, he will kick the shit out of you." I have to admit, I was a little pleased that he thought I would have the guts to go over to him. But he was right; there was no way I could... even if I had the bottle. "What you need is a little help from your Uncle John," he said, downing the rest of his half empty glass. "Are you finishing that?"

"Er, no."

"Well, we can't waste all of that, can we?" John smiled, taking the glass from my hand and downing it as quickly as he could. "I'm going to be belching and farting all fucking night but I'm sure you will live. Come on!"

John grabbed my arm and led me out of the pub. Back in the chill of the night air, I stopped.

"Where are we going?

"To my place!"

"Oh, that's really nice of you, but…"

"Look," John interrupted, "… if you want to get anywhere close to him, you're gonna need…" he hesitated, "… help," he smiled. "Come on."

***

As John opened the door to his flat, the light from the hallway spilled into his lounge. He rubbed the wall, clicking on the lounge light and walked in. I followed nervously behind. I don't know what I was expecting, I really don't. But it was just a normal, nicely furnished room. There was a large leather three piece suite which dominated one half of the lounge, with a dining table and four chars at the end, in front of some doors that lead out onto a balcony.

"First thing first, beer," he stated.

"I don't really drink," I smiled, embarrassed at having to admit it.

"You don't say!" he smiled. "I'll get you one anyway and you can take your time. But one way or another, you will bloody finish it!"

I said nothing. I just smiled and felt my face flush red. In no time, John was back with two cold cans of lager. He passed me one and opened his, quickly putting the can to his lips to save as much as possible from going over the laminate flooring.

"Go on. You can do it!" he encouraged.

I pulled the ring and took a large mouthful and then swallowed. It wasn't a taste I liked immediately but I got the impression that I would be having enough for the taste to grow on me. John placed his can down on a coffee table and took off his jacket, placing it down on a dining chair. My eyes were transfixed. His arms were covered in tattoos; so much so, I could hardly see any bare skin. Suddenly, this didn't seem like such a bad idea! John took a cigarette packet out of his jacket and lit one, before placing the packet and the lighter down on the table and picking up the can again.

"Now... where the fuck do I start with you?" he sighed, taking another lungful of smoke.

I sat down on the settee, partly to disguise how nervous I was but mostly because I was going weak at the knees at the sight of this man before me. There was not just one thing that grabbed my attention. It was a culmination of the light reflecting on his smooth shaved head, the ink etched into his slender but firm arms, the cigarette dangling from between his lips…. and, oh God… those boots.

"Get your kit off," John demanded.

"What? I'm not…."

"Get your clothes off. We need to get rid of that shit on your head. That will at least show me what else I need to do… plus, it would be a fucking start."

I stood up and removed my jacket, draping it on the settee. I started to unbutton the top button on my shirt when John shouted "For fuck sake Nick!" He walked towards me and I was bracing myself to get a smack. "Can I be honest? Well it don't really fucking matter, because I'm going to…this shirt is shit mate. It makes you look like your dad!" John grabbed my shirt and ripped it open. Buttons flew everywhere but he didn't look in the least concerned. "I have one you can have." John looked at me, still shell shocked. "Don't thank me or anything!"

"What? Sorry…. Thanks."

"Nick relax. Don't say thanks… try saying cheers. It will be a lot more… socially acceptable. Well, in my world anyway!"

"OK, then… cheers."

"That's more like it. You finish getting undressed mate and I will be back in a bit. And chill the fuck out!"

John left the room and I breathed a huge sigh of relief. I wanted so much to change. I wanted so much to try and be the man that John wanted me to be. But it wouldn't be easy. I was way out of my comfort zone… and then some! I sat down on the settee and removed my shoes and socks. I slid my trousers down and folded them neatly on the settee next me. And there I was, standing in a strange flat, more exposed than I had ever been in my life.

Eventually, John came back into the room, his cigarette grasped in his fingers while he held a pair of clippers.

"Not bad," he said, his eyes scanning me. "You'd have a good body if you firmed up a bit."

"Cheers," I smiled.

"Right. Let's do this. Grab that chair from the dining table and bring it over here for me."

I dutifully did as I was commanded and sat down. I jumped a little as I heard the clippers buzz into life.

"Right, now I'm going to clip this crap off and then, once it's off, you can wet shave it in the bathroom.

"Are you sure about this?"

"Definitely. If you wanna stand any chance with that….what was his name?"

"Pitch."

"Well remembered! Ready?"

"Go on then."

I stared straight ahead as the buzzing grew louder. In no time large chunks of my light brown hair were falling down my chest and onto my lap. I picked up a chunk of hair and gulped… no turning back now. I could feel the unguarded clippers running up from my neck, up the back and sides of my head. I thought it would feel like an eternity. In my mind, I imagined time would somehow be in slow motion as my hair dropped around my body. But in no time John was coming around the front and putting the finishing touches before flicking off the clippers and admiring his work.

"Fuck me!"

"What?" I gasped.

"Mate, you need to see yourself in the mirror. You look…… different."

"Good different?"

"I'm just sticking with different. To me you look shit-loads better. But for you, it will be a shock."

"Oh my God;" I almost whispered.

"It's fine. Come in the bathroom and I will wet shave it. Bring the chair!"

***

I picked up the chair and walked through to the bathroom. I wanted to know… I desperately wanted to see myself. But I also felt as though if I didn't look, it hadn't just happened. I eventually looked in the mirror and hardly recognised the man staring back at me. Well, it was definitely all off… and my ears didn't look like someone had left the car doors open, which I was grateful for.

"What do you think?" John asked, mostly out of politeness.

"You're right...it's different."

"Well, you're at the point of no return now mate. Let's just do this!"

I sat in silence, watching myself as John lathered my head. His inked arm reached around me, picking up the razor and I swallowed as I felt the metal against my scalp. It was only at that point I realised that he didn't have his cigarette any more. I hadn't notice him discard it and I wasn't about to mention it. I just watched as he worked on the back of my head. Suddenly I felt a sharp pain.

"Shit, I nicked your neck. It's not deep or bad. Sorry."

"It's fine. I'm just grateful for anything you can do for me."

John grabbed something from the shelf to my left. I didn't notice what, I assumed it was a plaster. I was just so transfixed on the sight in the mirror. But it wasn't a plaster… it was a small clear nicotine patch.

"There. Good as fucking new!" he smiled.

***

I felt so much better after a nice hot shower. I came into the lounge, wrapped in a white bathrobe and stopped as I saw John sitting on the settee. He had his jacket back on but his polo shirt had been removed, along with his bleachers. But his boots remained strapped to his legs. He looked amazing as his open jacket revealed more tattoos decorating his chest and stomach. I don't know if I felt empowered by the shaved head, or the lager from earlier (or the nicotine was beginning to kick in) but I walked across the lounge and sat down on the settee next to him.

"Like it?" John asked.

"Getting there thanks…er, cheers."

"That's better." John raised his hand and ran it over my smooth skin. "Feels amazing!"

"Does it?"

"Try mine!" he smiled. I lifted my hand ran it from front to back… it felt so good. "See?"

"Yeah. Oh yeah! So what next?"

"Are you a virgin?" John asked.

"No," I said defiantly and with conviction.

"OK, OK. I just wanted to know, to see what to do next. That's all."

A silence descended. An awkward silence where neither really knew what to say or where to go now. John lit another cigarette and I watched as the end glowed red.

"I'm not," I finally managed to mumble, my voice now lower and calmer. "OK, I haven't had a lot of experience sexually… but I'm not..."

"Sure. Maybe I was a little blunt." John took another drag on his cigarette. "So what experience do you have of the whole master and slave thing?"

"Sorry?"

"Master and slave. You have heard of it, right?" I looked away, embarrassed at my naivety. "Right, looks like we will have to go back to basics. Masters and slaves is basically exactly what it says on the tin. One, the master, likes the feeling of controlling another person. The other, the slave, like's to be controlled."

"How do you mean control?"

"OK, well…the master might tell the slave to lick his boots. A lot of people, both masters and slaves, like that!"

"Yeah?"

"Fuck yeah. It's horny as fuck!"

"And which are you?"

"I'm mainly bottom. That means I like to get fucked."

"Oh right."

"But seeing as this is a crash training course, I suppose I could get a bit bossy… if you like?"

"Well, in the name of research I suppose we should," I grinned.

"Get on your fucking knees!" John smiled.

I slid myself off of the settee and knelt down in front of him. John's tattooed fingers fumbled with his black underpants and in no time, his semi hard cock flopped in front of me. I went to open my mouth but John stopped me.

"Nicky-boy, there is no rush mate! Sometimes, less is more."

"I don't understand."

"OK. You get back up here and I will show you."

I sat back on the settee and John untied the belt of the bathrobe. He leant forward but instead of taking me in his mouth, he kissed my belly and ran his tongue sensually around it. His tongue made circuits around my cock, almost tickling the inside of my crutch, gently running under my balls but never touching my cock. The pleasuring torment seemed to last for ages. Then, when his opened his mouth and took me inside, I felt like a volcano erupting. After barely a few strokes of his mouth, John looked up at me.

"Now get the idea?"

"I do. I totally do!"

"Your turn!"

"Get on the floor," I requested.

John stood up, his pierced cock now hard and standing to attention. He sat on the floor, sighing as he lay down. I straddled his legs and started to kiss the large cross tattooed around his belly button. I ran my tongue around his crotch but as his pubes had been shaved off, it seemed extra sensual… well, for me anyway. I ran my tongue up his body bypassing his chest and onto his neck. John moved his head to the side as my tongue caressed the 'Die Young' tattoo on his neck. I could feel him take another drag on his cigarette and it felt so erotic. I pushed his face up to look at me again just as he exhaled. His smoke curled around me and although it made me cough a little, I just wanted to take him there and then.

"Get back to work, you little cunt," John growled. I put my tongue down on his breast bone and slowly glided it over his smooth, hairless chest to his pierced nipple. "Good boy. Fuck that feels so good." John reached over to the side of the settee and grabbed a large dildo. "I'm going to fuck you boy. I'm going to make a man out of you!" But my eyes were closed as I clasped his nipple in my mouth. Plus, I had no idea what he meant!

As my lips released the metal through his nipple, John's cock strained. I could feel his pierced knob rubbing my tight hole. I leant forward again and grasped the other nipple firmly between my lips. I could feel the metal under the skin and it excited me even further. It was at that moment I knew I was doing the right thing. When I had been sitting alone in the office just hours earlier, I never had thought, even dreamed, this could be possible. My lips released John's nipple and I grasped it gently between my teeth. John's back arched and he groaned with pleasure. Gently but firmly, I moved my lower jaw from side to side, almost rolling his nipple between my teeth.

"Oh fuck!" he shouted.

I lowered my arse down and John's cock head gently kissed my hole. I lowered myself slowly and his pierced knob started to disappear inside me. But John did not even notice. His hand gripped the rubber dildo so hard that his knuckles were turning white, as my teeth continued to chew on his nipple. With his eyes closed and his mouth open, John was lost to the world. There could have been an elephant running through the lounge of his flat and he wouldn't have noticed. The only thing on John's mind was the pleasure he was receiving... and he loved it.

It was only when I released his nipple and sat right down on his cock that John returned to what was happening.

"What are you doing? No!"

"Oh my God. This is amazing."

"No Nick, stop. I usually don't normally...!" but his words tailed off.

I looked down at him and grabbed the dildo from his hand. I reached around and started to rub the helmet on his hole. John spread his legs a little and continued to protest. But I was having the time of my life and was there was no way I was giving up this cock. I began to feed the dildo into him and he gasped with a mixture of pain and pleasure. I could feel his cock throb inside me as it slid inside him.

"Oh fuck... you little cunt."

"Fuck me John! Fuck me!"

John took another drag on his cigarette. I grabbed the ashtray from the arm of the settee and placed it on the floor next to him and he stubbed out the finished cigarette.

"Have another one!" I pleaded.

"No!"

"John please," I begged, "Have another one!"

I passed him his cigarettes and as he took one from the packet, I clasped the dido and began to fuck him again. I was now riding him hard and loving every minute. My arse slide up his shaft, the bottom of his PA almost coming out of me, then straight back down until my arse cheeks could feel his bollocks hanging out of me. I was in ecstasy feeling the metal of his PA scouring my insides. John dragged on his cigarette and smoke once again curled around me. As I moved my hole up and down his shaft harder and faster, my strokes with the dildo matched my pace.

"Swear at me. Talk dirty to me," I begged.

"Ram that dildo as I fuck you, you bastard! Fuck it feels so good. You like having this bonehead bastard inside you?"

"Yes mate. I love it."

"Call me Boss you little cunt!"

"Yes Boss. Fuck me!"

"You love taking my fucking skinhead shaft?"

"Yes Boss."

"Come on boy; fuck me hard with that fake cock!"

John took another drag on his cigarette and blew the smoke over me again. I was in heaven. My body was in overdrive and my senses were in uncharted territory. The culmination of having this shaved, tattooed man inside me, the sweat glistening on his tattooed body, the smoke and the swearing was driving me to the edge, escalated as John released a loud burp.

"John I'm getting close!"

"Yeah? Come on, fucking cum on me. Soak me with your cum, cunt!"

"John…."

"Cunt… come on you cunt… dirty little cunt. Cum on me!"

"So close," I whimpered, almost raping his solid meat.

"Cunt. You dirty little cunt!" John continued.

I threw my head back and closed my eyes. I forced my arse down as far as I could, as my cock blasted my cum up John's glistening body. The first few spurts hit his chest, then as the intensity began to subside, it reached further down his torso. The black cross was splattered with spots of white and a puddle of cum filled his belly button right in the middle of it. Once the last of my spunk had been released, we both panted hard. But I didn't once stop moving my arse up and down his thick meat. I began to pick up the pace again, ramming the dildo harder and harder and savouring the feeling of his cock still buried inside me.

"Oh fuck, now it's my turn! Make me cum boy. Make me fucking cum!"

I worked as hard as I could. I was euphoric, impaled on his hard pierced shaft, my balls empty and trying desperately to make him cum.

"I'm so fucking close."

I let go of the dildo and left it inside him. I leant forward and kissed his lips. Our tongues wrestled as my arse continued to work on his dick. I ran my fingers over his soft smooth scalp. John put his hand on my chest and pushing me up. I writhed on top of him as he panted.

"I'm gonna cum. I'm gonna fucking cum"

"Come on Boss, cum inside me, you bastard."

I don't know why I said it. I wasn't one to swear normally. But these were not normal times. In the space of a few hours, my while life and everything I thought I knew about myself had been blown into a million pieces. I had not only entered the forbidden sanctum of the pub but I had had my head shaved and was now being fucked senseless by a booted, tattooed skinhead.

"I'm fucking cumming!" he bellowed.

He forced his cock as deep as he could. He groaned with pleasure as his cock erupted inside me. I too gasped as I felt his shaft pulse as he pumped his thick white seed deep inside me. I flopped down on top of him, his cock still inside me and the dildo still inside him. I moved gently in rhythmic synchronicity with his chest as he panted beneath me.

"Well," John gasped. "That… is the end… of the first… lesson. Fuck…ing… hell!" he panted, resting his head on his arm as the other raised his cigarette to his lips again.

Part Two

Saturday

It was late Saturday morning when my eyes flickered open. The bed was dishevelled. The duvet was half way down the bed, with most of it on the floor. I looked over and watched as John slept. I looked down and saw he was still wearing his boots. I looked up at the ceiling, trying to process everything that had happened just as John began to stir.

"Morning!" was all I could manage to say.

"Morning," he replied.

"I have a confession," I started, stopping and swallowing hard. "I lied yesterday… I was a virgin!"

John swung his boots over the edge of the bed and stood up.

"Fuck. It's been an awful long time since I stole anyone's cherry, I can tell ya!" he said, standing up and walking out to the bathroom. "My cunt is fucking sore. You really rammed that dildo didn't ya?"

As he walked, I watched the scorpion tattoo on his arse as he strolled naked except for the boots. The sound of a steady stream of piss filled the room. I smiled to myself, lying alone in his bed just listening. Soon the toilet flushed and John reappeared.

"Can you remember where I put my fags?"

"No. I think they might still be in the lounge?"

"Fuck," he groaned and walked out of the bedroom.

***

In no time, John returned, a plume of smoke trailing behind him across the bedroom as he climbed back into bed.

"John?"

"What mate," he replied, clicking on the mobile he had brought in with him and checking for messages.

"Do you regret last night?"

"No mate, you stupid cunt! Why would I regret it?"

"I don't know."

"I'm the one who invited you back wasn't I?"

"Yeah I know, but…."

"Well then. Shut up and stop being a stupid bastard!" he said, looking back at his phone and taking a large drag on his cigarette.

"Do you think that bloke will be at the pub tonight?"

"I don't know mate. I wouldn't have thought so. I know there is some skinhead night across town tonight; he will probably be going to that. I was, but… well, I'm not now. He usually goes to the pub Sunday lunchtime. I doubt he will go out Sunday night as most people have work on Monday morning."

"I see!" I said.

"I'm only supposing but by my thinking, we have until tomorrow lunch to get your ready."

"So we will need to cram in a lot more training?" I smiled.

"That's what I mean mate."

"Well, no time to start like the present," I grinned, reaching over to grab his cock.

"There's plenty of time for that! I want you to do something for me first."

"Like what?" I asked, nervously.

"Lick my fucking boots."

"What?"

"Look mate, if this guy does want to fuck you and he asks you to do something, he is gonna expect you to do it…" John said, looking up from his phone, "… not have a fucking debate about it. Just keep your eyes on the prize and do as you're fucking told! Now, lick my fucking boots!"

I pushed the remaining duvet off my legs and crawled down the bed. I leant down and placed my face close to the black, 30 hole boot. The scent entered my nostrils. I stuck out my tongue, hesitant but strangely drawn. I lowered my head and my tongue touched his boot, gently flicking. I don't know what I was expecting. I suppose I thought it would taste disgusting, or I would have dirt and bits of grit stuck to my tongue. But it wasn't like that at all. It was smooth and sensual, nothing like I had imagined. I looked up the boots towards John's face. The cigarette was between his lips and he was still texting on his phone, seemingly hardly paying attention. But the twitching of his cock betrayed him.

With my confidence boosted and safe in the knowledge that John liked it, I began to relax. I ran my tongue down, further and further until I reached the foot. It glided along the side and over the toes before beginning its ascent back up. My tongue crossed the white laces and slid up the other side of the boot. I was beginning to get a little impatient. I wanted to continue up the boot and onto the bare skin of his leg. I wanted to feel his skin quiver as the sensual feeling, rose up his leg, onto his balls and then onto his cock. I wanted so desperately to taste him, have him inside my mouth and relish the feeling. But I didn't. I may not be the sharpest tool in the box but I understand that when John says 'do as you're told'… that is exactly what you do. So once my tongue reached the top of the boot, it briefly touched his skin, before working its way back down. While my tongue worked on one boot, my hand caressed the other. My fingers felt the smoothness of the boot around his calf and skin, the creases at the ankle and the firmness on the foot and toes.

John reached down and grabbed me hard by my ear. He said nothing but pulled me up towards him. He let go of my ear and pushed my face into his hairless crotch. I could smell a mixture of sweat and piss as John held my face there, my nose buried by his balls. Then he released the pressure and began to stroke my smooth scalp. I took the opportunity, opened my mouth and closed my lips around his semi hard meat. It was everything I had wanted it to be. I could feel his cock stiffen as my tongue rubbed the end of his knob and flicked the ball of his piercing. My lips slide down his shaft… down and down… inch by inch, until my lips were touching the smooth skin where his pubes use to be. I choked as the metal touched the back of my throat. My eyes watered before I slowly slid my lips back up his thick erect dick. John took another large lungful of smoke as my head bobbed up and down between his legs. He watched, his eyes transfixed and his hand stroking my scalp until his mobile beeped. He picked up his phone and began to text, just enjoying me take every inch of him. Without warning his cock spurted its contents in my mouth, hitting the back of my mouth and taking me completely by surprise. I swallowed the thick warm liquid which clung to the back of my throat.

"Fucking hell, that was good!" I smiled, wiping my mouth with the back of my hand.

"One load up your cunt and another pumped down your throat. You lucky fucker!"

***

Saturday slipped past. The only time training did not continue was when John sent me to the shop for cigarettes and some more lager. The temperature had plummeted and as I closed the front door behind me and walked into the lounge, I saw John lying on the sheep skin rug in front of a roaring fire. He had a leather harness strapped across his chest, a flimsy leather waist coat and leather chaps covering his legs.

"Fuck…me," I said slowly.

"I thought you would say that!" John replied.

He reached under the rug and brought out another dildo, an evil grin spread across his face. I put the bag down on the floor and took off my jacket. I unbuttoned the borrowed shirt that John had given me and wrapped it around the back of a dining chair.

"We should think about getting you inked," John smiled.

"Really? Like what?"

"Well, once we bulk you up a bit, we can think about that. Maybe something small in the meantime… swallows? Something like that."

As my jeans dropped the floor, John took a cigarette out of the packet. He lit it from the fire as I walked over.

"I'll be glad when this is over and you have fucked off. I have never smoked so much in my fucking life," John smirked.

"You love it," I grinned. Kneeling down with my hands and knees either side, moving up his body.

"Maybe!"

As I reached his chest, I immediately started sucking on his nipple. I wasn't sure if it was the feeling, or the memory of before (or a culmination of the two) but his cock started to twitch again and I knew I was on the right track. John's hand held the back of my head, pushing my face onto him harder and harder. Once again I clasped him between my teeth, gently biting with a little increasing pressure. I slid my fingers down his smooth flat stomach and grasped his stiff shaft in my hand. John gasped, closing his eyes and tilting his head back in ecstasy. After minutes almost drowning in intoxication, he grabbed my ears and pulled me to his face.

"Turn around and suck me!" he whispered.

The glow from the fire seemed to brighten as I turned around. I lay next to him on the soft rug and took his hard on into my mouth. John gasped, and then I felt smoke hit my body as he exhaled over me again. His hands gripped my arse cheeks, slipping his tattooed middle finger in my arse and I sank into pleasure. As my mouth worked on his thick hard tool, John's finger worked its magic on my hole. I took this as instruction and gently inserted my finger into his crack.

"Yes... fuck yes," I heard him almost whisper.

With my other hand, I tenderly ran my fingers down the bottom of his spine and up his back as far as I could. My fingers were barely touching his skin, causing a tingle to run across his body. His back was incredibly hot and it was not long before John rolled towards me, eventually lying with his full weight on top of me. As his balls dropped down onto my face, my spare hand gripped the leather strap at the top of his leather chaps as John finally took me into his mouth. The image of the scorpion tattoo on his arse returned to the forefront of my mind. Just knowing that his inked arse cheek was now on top of me, moving his cock up and down my throat was such a turn on but then all his tattoos were a turn on. His shaved head was a turn on and especially him smoking was a turn on.

We stayed in the 69 position for a while, just exploring and tasting each other's bodies. Then John rolled off of me, panting.

"Do you want me to use the dildo?" I asked.

"Yeah but plenty of lube mate."

"Move around then," I asked.

"There is a sucker on the end mate. Stick it to the floor!"

I pushed the end down onto the laminate flooring, and after a couple of attempts, it stuck fast. I broke open a small packet of lube and emptied the whole sachet onto the dildo. John stood up and squatted down onto it, very gingerly. My eyes widened as I watched the black rubber dildo inch its way up into his body. Eventually, virtually all of it had disappeared. John knelt down, his boot clad legs now resting on the floor, his eyes closed, a smile flickering on his face in a mixture of pain and pleasure. John took another large drag on his cigarette and exhaled. The nicotine patch on the back of my neck was now empty and the need for more began to consume me.

"John?"

"What mate," he said, his eyes remaining closed.

"Could I try a fag?"

"Help yourself," he gasped.

I took a cigarette from his packet and lit it. It made me cough as I swallowed the smoke. It was only then that John opened his eyes and egged me on to take another, which I did. I knelt down in front of John and kissed his lips. We both ran our fingers over each other heads as our tongues tussled. I didn't mean to but I pushed back slightly. He took his hand from my head and put it down on the floor to steady himself. We stopped kissing and John placed the nearly finished cigarette back between his lips. He wanked his cock hard, his eyes remaining closed and his breathing heavy.

"Fuck I'm getting close," John said, blowing out another plume of smoke from his nostrils.

I stood up quickly and then squatted down on John's hard, swollen tool. It had barely got in when I felt his cock pumping. I pushed it in deeper and deeper and it slid easily, lubricated with his own spunk.

"You're such a bastard," he said, opening his eyes. I smiled and stood up and John gingerly rose to his feet too. "Now it's your turn!"

John pushed me down onto the rug and placed my hand down onto my cock, forcing me to wank. I felt the softness of the wool and the warmth of the fire, and his fresh hot spunk beginning to trickle out of my fucked hole. I closed my eyes and my imagination instantly took me back to the feeling of John's cock back inside me. How I loved that feeling… the feeling of being full of his cock. The feeling of the metal ball from his piercing deep inside me as his cock blasted his thick cum. I gasped in pleasure and my breathing intensified. John lowered himself down onto me and my eyes opened wide. The feeling was weird and I didn't really like it… this confirmed I was a definite bottom but it didn't stop me cumming inside him.

Both our bodies glistened with sweat as John lay next to me on the rug. He took the cigarette from my fingers and put it to his lips.

"Now that was fucking awesome!" he smiled.

***

The rest of the day passed quickly. We maintained the training, working on my attitude, swearing and making sure everything would be as good as it could for tomorrow.

Part 3

Sunday

After a night on the lager, we both woke up late on Sunday morning. We shared a packet of Aspirin and tried to compose ourselves as today...was D Day!

11.45 and we strolled down the street towards the pub. I was dressed in John's clothes and boots and was beginning to feel a little self-conscious. Back in the security of John's flat, the whole transformation from pathetic nothing to a skin had felt really positive. Cocooned in there, everything had been safe… had been nerve racking but only from trying new experiences. Now, on show to the world (and people I knew) I felt extremely exposed. But I tried my best to stride down the road, looking as comfortable as I could, even if it was for John's sake. I kept running it over in my mind. If I could just talk to Pitch... If I could just make him look at me and even have a conversation then I would have regarded this whole weekend as a success.

John however had other plans. After this unplanned weekend where let's face it both of our boundaries had been pushed, nothing would be satisfactory unless I left with Pitch. He was not prepared to settle for second best. This was all or nothing! He was not prepared to have not wasted his time or been imposed on all weekend for just a conversation. No fucking way!

***

As we opened the pub door, we were instantly met with a wall of bodies. The pub was heaving and it took a long time just to get to the bar.

"Is he here?" John asked, as he ordered the drinks.

"I can't see" I replied. Suddenly, I caught a glimpse of him across the other side of the pub. "I think I can see him!"

The crowd jostled and both John and I were having trouble keeping Pitch in sight.

"I really appreciate everything you have done," I smiled.

"Nick, you're a lovely guy and I really like you, but…don't take this the wrong… I never fucking wanna go through that again!" I laughed, half thinking he was joking but still wondering if there was an element of truth. "Are you going to go and talk to him?"

"And say what?"

"Come on Nick. I have taught you how to look, how to act, how to dress and even how to fuck... Do I really need to tell you what to say?"

"Well, I…"

"Look where he is standing, it is right en-route to the toilets. Go for a piss!" John encouraged.

I took a large sip of my drink and began to fight my way through the crowd. John watched as I slipped between groups of talking people and watched their expressions once I had passed. Most looked on as I continued and little groups made comments. As I reached Pitch, John took another sip of his pint. John's heart was almost in his mouth as I grew closer and closer. As I reached him, John watched as I smiled and brushed past him. John could almost see Pitch's mind ticking over. Pitch sipped his pint as his eyes followed me, the expression on his face was obvious… was that him?

Time ticked past and I eventually came out of the toilet. John smiled: he knew I had been waiting in there to see if Pitch would come in… but he hadn't. I edged closer and closer towards Pitch and John watched. "Go on Nick, say something! Fucking say something!" As I reached Pitch, we smiled at each other and I sidled past, without saying anything. "Fuck" John muttered as he took another sip of his drink. He was just about to look away when he saw Pitch call me back. I had my back to John, who could only read Pitch's face to guage what was going on. Pitch looked over and stared directly at him. John's heart nearly stopped, 'What the fuck is he saying?' he thought to himself.

John looked away, his mind racing. He swallowed hard as different scenarios ran through his mind. As his mind raced, he felt a hand on his shoulder. He turned around to see Pitch standing before him.

"Get your fucking arse outside. Now!"

***

As I waited outside, I shuffled in the cold. I watched as my warm breath condensed in the cold air and I was instantly transported back to being a child, pretending I was smoking. Suddenly, I jolted forward as I was pushed from behind, falling to the floor and hitting my head on the pavement.

"You fucking faggot. You should all be fucking put down at birth."

I looked up and saw a man standing there, his fists clenched and hatred burning in his eyes. He had shaved hair at the sides which was longer on the top, with a dark moustache and a long thick coat, jeans and trainers.

"What the fuck?" I said, getting to my feet.

"You lot are like a disease," he continued.

"Who are you?" I stammered, fear almost making me unable to speak.

"I am the man that you faggots have to fear," he snarled.

Suddenly, there was a tap on his shoulder.

"And I am the man you fucking straights have to fear!"

The man turned around to see Pitch and John standing in front him. Without warning, Pitch head butted him and the man's nose exploded. Blood spurted, splattering Pitch's face as the man dropped the floor.

"Get up, you fucking narrow minded wanker!" John barked.

"Mate, you have to be a gentleman and help him up," Pitch said softly.

John grabbed the man by the coat and with the help of Pitch almost lifted him back to his feet. Pitch pulled back his fist and BAM… smacked him in the face. Pitch could feel the jaw shatter beneath the man's skin and again the man dropped to the concrete ground. Both Pitch and John kicked their boots into him as his body writhed around on the ground in pain.

Eventually, the kicking subsided and Pitch and John stood looking down at him, panting. Pitch was about to wipe the blood from his face with the back of his jacket sleeve.

"No don't mate. It's war paint!" John smiled.

"Go on Nick, you get a few in," Pitch smiled.

"What?"

"Go on mate, fill yer boots!"

"Go on Nick. Pretend it's your Boss!" John goaded.

I moved around and stood between John and Pitch. I looked down and with a little imagination, I saw my boss's face lying on the ground before me. That was all the reason I needed. I drew back the borrowed cherry boot and kicked him in the stomach. Suddenly all the resentment and hatred flooded out. It was like the cap of a shaken fizzy bottle had been released and everything came out. After a while, it still looked like I wasn't going to stop. John wrapped his arms around me and pulled me away. Pitch picked up the unconscious bleeding heaped on the floor, and put him over his shoulder.

"What are you doing?" John asked.

"I'm not done with him yet! We need to teach this wanker a lesson!"

"Pitch, is this a good idea?" I muttered.

"No one picks on my mates! We'll take him to Nick's… it's closer" John smiled.

Thankfully, there was no one around as we walked the short distance to my flat.

***

Back at my flat, we hurried inside so as not to be seen. Pitch dropped the bloke on the floor before he and John sat down on my settee.

"Got any beers?"

"No. I… I have to get some" I lied.

"Well, you run off like a good boy and let the men sort this out!" Pitch snarled.

I turned around and closed the front door behind me.

***

When I returned, John and Pitch were sitting back on the settee, while the man (now awake) was tied to my dining chair. He had a real look of terror in his eyes as he bit down on a tea towel tied around his mouth. I passed Pitch and John a cold can that I got from the fridge in the shop on the corner, before placing the other cans in the fridge.

"So, what are going to do with his little fucker?" John asked

"Just let him go" I said, a little scared that he was in my flat.

"Fuck that. This little weasel needs to be taught a fucking lesson" Pitch protested.

"What are you going to do?" I asked, nervously.

"Well this little shit hates gays, so I suggest we show him exactly what we get up to!"

"Get up to?" I asked, showing myself up.

"I think we should fuck in front of him!" Pitch said, spelling it out for my benefit.

John looked over at me and my gaze flicked between him, Pitch and the guy.

"I'm really not…."

"What's the matter?" Pitch interrupted.

"Sure, why not?" I smiled. "It will teach him a thing or two!"

"Are you sure mate?" John pressed.

"Sure. But I have to go to the toilet, so you two go for it" I said, walking out of the room.

"What the fuck was all that about?" Pitch asked, bewildered.

"How long have you got mate?" John stated.

***

I sat in the toilet alone, feeling like my life was going out of control. There I was, my life completely transformed. The man I had been fretting over was sitting in my flat and I was sitting in the bloody toilet on my own. "Come on Nick, pull yourself together" I said to myself.

***

Back in the lounge, John's body rocked as Pitch pushed hard into him.

"So, you have been teaching him?" Pitch said.

"You saw the state of him on Friday night. What else could I do?"

"Did you fuck him?" Pitch asked, his body stopping and his eyes burning into John's very soul.

John remained calm on the outside. But inside his mind was racing. What should he say? Should he admit everything or make Pitch think he was the first?

"He was a virgin… Wouldn't you?" John eventually said.

There was a silence, a tense silence that lasted a matter of seconds but felt like an hour.

"Too fucking right," Pitch laughed, and continued thrusting.

***

When I returned to the lounge undressed, John was leaning against the sideboard with Pitch behind him. John glanced over and I smiled, just to reassure him that I was comfortable with everything. He smiled and I could see him physically relax and begin to enjoy himself.

My eyes locked onto Pitch. Back then, he didn't have nearly as many tattoos as he has now. But the ones he had were bright and fresh. His head was shaved smooth and he watched himself in the mirror as he fucked. Apart from looking at me on my return, his eyes flicked between his reflection in the mirror and the man tied to the chair.

"Are you watching? You little shit!" Pitch snarled to the man, still tied to the chair. "Watch me! Watch as I cum up his cunt!"

As he came, Pitch rammed his cock as deep as he could. John's body jolted, gasping in pleasure, before his movements subsided and Pitch pulled out. Pitch walked over to the man, his cock still hard and dripping, and the man struggled and shook his head in fear. John placed his arse by the man's face and farted. Thick white cum sprayed on the man's face and the flat erupted with laughter. I laughed so hard that my sides began to ache.

As the laughter died down, Pitch beckoned me forward. This was it. This was the moment I had been dreaming of the whole time I had been at John's. I took the same place as John had before and Pitch pushed his cock hard inside me. I cried out as he started to fuck me hard, balancing on tiptoe as he was so much taller than me at the time. John watched, grabbing the man by the hair and lifting his head to make him watch.

"Keep watching boy!" Pitch snarled at the man. "If you're really unlucky… you could be next!" he laughed.

I closed my eyes and bit my tongue. I loved the feeling of Pitch inside me but with everything else that had happened over the weekend, the pain was intense. When Pitch pulled out of me, I was more than a little relieved. Pitch lay down on the carpet and I straddled him, slowly sliding my cunt down his pierced shaft again. It was easier in this position as I was in more control of the depth and speed of the thrusting.

"Light me a fag will ya?" Pitch asked.

John lit two cigarettes and passed one to Pitch. The excitement built inside me again as he smoked. At that moment, everything else seemed to fade into insignificance. The world outside ceased to exist… even John and this wretched man evaporated. There was only me and Pitch. I felt ecstasy flood over me as his hard shaft sliced through my body. His large rough hands ran up my flat belly and onto my chest as I rode his dick harder and faster, as I had with John.

"I'm gonna cum. I'm gonna fucking cum again," He bellowed.

Pitch pushed his hard shaft as deep as he could. I shuddered with pleasure as I felt his cock pumping thick jets of sperm inside me. Suddenly we were alone no more. John and the man reappeared in my consciousness and the situation with the hostage resumed.

Part 4

Monday

As I woke on Monday morning, I swung my legs over the edge of my king-size bed. I had never needed a king size bed and if I'm honest, I don't know why I bought it. But now I was glad I had. I looked back and saw John was on the opposite side with Pitch lying in between us. John stirred at the same time as me but Pitch was already awake.

"Oh fuck...that bloke. He has been tied to the chair all fucking night!" I shouted.

"Relax, he has gone," Pitch said casually.

"Gone?" I asked. "Fuck, we are in so much trouble."

"It's sorted. Last night, while you two slept with my spunk swimming around your guts, I stuck him in the boot on my car and drove him down to Brighton."

"You drove from London to Brighton and back?" John asked.

"And left him there?" I asked.

"I sure did. I left him tied to a park bench in just his under crackers. That will teach the little wanker to pick on us. I told him that if I ever saw him in London again, I would make last night look like a picnic. There won't be any repercussions."

***

Later that morning, the door to the office burst open. My manager, Mr. Jefferson, didn't even look up.

"Well, well. Nice of you to turn up, three...hours...late. I don't think I need to tell you the trouble you are in. Your wages will be docked and I expect no trouble from you at all today. Do I make myself clear?"

I gave no reply. As Mr. Jefferson looked up, his eyes widened at the changed man that stood before him. I leant forward and hit him as hard as I could in the face. The force knocked him out of his chair and onto the floor. I had been waiting so long to do that! I calmly turned around and boldly strode up through the office and out of the door, slamming it closed behind me.

Getting inked

We walked in to the tattooist and you stand by the chair. He smiles, as he recalls the last time we were there.

"You're here for two swallows on your neck, right Pitch?"

"That's right!"

"And what will you be doing during this session? You had your finger up his arse while I was inking your knob!"

"I know," you grinned. "Well that's all healed now and it's a shame to have it and not use it now isn't it?" you smile.

"I got ya mate," the tattooist grinned, shaking his head.

You pull off your polo shirt and start to undo you bleachers before pulling them down. I stair in admiration at the tat on your cock as your pa glistens in the light.

"Strip then, you little cunt," you bark, as you climb into the chair.

I strip naked, still a little embarrassed at the presence of the tattooist, even though he has seen it all before. I kneel down and start to run my tongue down your already semi hard cock, down your shaft and onto your full bollocks. You can feel the warmth of my breath touching your skin and I savour the taste of your cock. Then I run my tongue back up to your twitching shaft … up, up to my main prize, your new inked knob.

"Are you ready Pitch?" the tattooist asked.

"Hang on a minute," you say, still looking down at me." I open my mouth and take you inside. Your cock responds to the warm wet mouth as I start to slide my lips down your cock. "OK, you can start now," you say.

I can hear the tattoo gun start as my lips continue their descent, until they reach your bollocks. My cock twitches as I begin to imagine what is happening out of sight. I gag as your hard cock lodges in my throat.

"Fucking hell. Is he alright?" the tattooist asks.

"Who cares? He is fine. Aren't you Nick!"

I can't say anything. I nod, and slowly begin to bring my lips back up your solid meat.

"Getting inked and getting blown, it can't get much better than that."

"Oh it can mate," you smile. "And it fucking will!"

My head bobs up and down on your shaft as the needle forced the black ink of the outline into your neck. I'm desperate to watch. I wanna see you getting inked again so badly it almost hurts. But I know my time will come….sooner or later! But for now, I can not desert my post. I know what is good for me! So I keep sucking on your dick.

"OK mate, that's the outline done."

"Good. Now the fun can really start! Oi, cunt… get up here." I stand up, my cock hard as I gaze at the black outline on your neck. "Get that fucking cunt on my cock. I'm gonna fuck you as I'm getting coloured in."

I struggle to climb up on the chair. I straddle you and rub the swallow tattooed on your knob and the metal ring against my hole. You look down and watch as the word SKINHEAD down your cock disappears letter by letter inside me. Fuck it feels so good... seeing you laying there, your previous tats on full display, new ink being carved into your neck but better still, ink and metal inside me. I gasp as your cock slices through my guts until I have your full length inside me.

"Fucking hell, he loves it," the tattooist, smiles as he sorts the colours.

"Of course he fucking does. I'm all he wants. I'm his fucking skinhead stud mate. He is so fucking tight...he has clamped my dick so much he might take the ink off," you laugh.

The tattooist laughs as he pushes your head to one side again and dips the needle into the first colour. As the sound of the gun starts again, I am so fucking turned on. Not only am I getting fucked by you but I'm getting fucked with your inked dick and knob, while you're getting another on your neck. I close my eyes and savour the feeling as I raise my hole up your hard shaft. I open my eyes as my hole nears your knob. I hover, your cock still just inside me… then, as the tattooist stops to dip the needle again, I drop down the full length of you cock.

"ARGH FUCK" you shout.

"Does it hurt?" he asks

"No, it's this fucking cunt. It feels so fucking good."

As the tattooist keeps working, I pick up the pace. My hole is moving firmly but steadily so as not to make him fuck up. Seeing beads of sweat glistening on your smooth scalp, your tattooed body moving gently as I'm milking your inked dick, is driving me fucking mental.

"Right, all done for that one mate!" the tattooist smiles, wiping the fresh new work. I stop fucking and just sit; your solid meat buried full length inside me. "I'm going out for a smoke before I do the other one on the other side."

"OK mate. We will just carry on. You don't mind if I smoke here do ya?"

"You shouldn't but you're the last appointment of the day, so I don't mind"

"Right you little cunt, pass me my fags," you growl as the tattooist walks out. I reach over and get your cigarettes and lighter. You light one and place them down on the floor. "Now he has stopped you can fuck me properly, can't you?"

"Yes."

"Yes what?"

"Yes sir."

"That's better." I start riding your cock again, harder and faster now the restriction has been removed. I wince and your cock pushes through my body. "You love getting fucked by this big skinhead cunt, don't you boy!"

"Yes. Oh fuck yes."

"Of course you do." You take a large drag on your cigarette and then blow the smoke over me. It curls around my body then you gob on my face. It runs down and part goes into my mouth while the rest drips onto my chest and slides down my body. "Come on, rape my fucking inked cock you bastard!"

I pick up the pace again and my hole is slamming down your dick. I lean forward and rub your smooth head and you take over the fucking. You take another drag on your cigarette and belch out the smoke.

"Oh fuck I'm gonna cum soon." I sit back up and take control again. "I'm gonna fill you with my fucking cum you dirty little cunt." At this moment the world did not exist. Nothing else mattered except the sex and me milking every last sperm from your full, heavy bollocks. "I'm fucking cumming," you shout, as you push your cock deep and it explodes inside me. I can feel your cock pumping as thick white jets of skinhead cum, spurts your DNA inside me, hitting the walls of my insides.

I can hold back no longer and spurt my cum over chest and belly.

"Oh you dirty bastard. You'll have to lick that of now, you fucker," you laugh.

With your cock still inside me, I lick up my mess from you. You lay panting as the tattooist returns.

"Alright mate?" He asks.

"For now," you reply.

I stand up and the tattooist sees your cum begin to run from my arse. He smiles to himself as he places himself on the other side of you.

"I take it you will be doing all that again this side mate?" the tattooist laughs.

"Of course," you smile, taking another drag of satisfaction on your cigarette.

TAT IT AGAIN

I push the front door closed with my foot and drop my cases on the floor in the hall. At that moment, my phone buzzes.

'Are you home? I need a quickie!" I read.

'Just got back,' I text.

'5' came the reply.

***

True to your word, in five minutes, my spare key was in the lock and you opened the door to my house, to see me with my jeans around my knees, leaning on the third step of my stairs.

"What's this? You on the naughty step or something?"

"No. You said you wanted a quickie."

"No, you daft cunt," You smile, "I'm getting quickie tattoos!"

"Oh... oh I see."

"Still, seeing as I'm here and you're like that, I could play glove puppets"

You walk over and put you middle finger in your mouth, pulling it out between your lips before pushing it in my tight hole. I jolt as you push, gasping with pleasure.

"Yeah Nick, that's what I have fucking missed."

You turn your hand, while pushing your middle finger in and out... in then out. You run the end around my hole before pushing it back inside me and making me gasp again. You then position your finger on my prostate and begin to massage it. I cry out again in pleasure as you other hand slaps my arse cheek

"Fuck yeah. You bloody love it, don't you, ya cunt?"

"Yes. Fuck yes."

"Well you'll have to wait," you say, stopping the massaging and pulling out your finger. "We have to go!"

***

We walk into the tattooist again and you remove your Fred Perry polo shirt. My eyes scanned your body. I have spent the last two weeks away, thinking of you. And now I'm back, the real thing is so much better than my imagination ever was. You drop your bleachers and climb in the chair, already playing with yourself.

"Swallows on your hands isn't it?"

"Yeah mate. Just by the thumbs. Both hands!"

"So what foreplay will you be getting him to do today?"

"None mate. We did that before we got here."

"Briefly," I muttered under my breath, pulling down my jeans.

"Come over here and get your leg over! Face away from me." you bark.

I'm not happy about having to face away from you but I do as I'm instructed. You look down and watch as your swallow vanishes… then D…A…E and H. "Stop," you shout and I hover on your cock. You savour the sight of the visible half of your inked cock, your eyes running up and down your shaft before you tell me to start again and watch the other letters disappear one by one.

Once your cock is in me full length, the tattooist places your hands down to start work.

"Hang on. Oi… turn round and face me. Now!" I didn't need telling twice. With your cock still inside me, I slowly managed to turn around, and then the tattooist started work. I can feel your cock twitch as the needle slices into your skin. "This is gonna look fucking excellent when it's done mate," you smile.

I start to move my tight arse on your thick hard skinhead meat. Sliding it to the top until the base of the swallows wing is visible… then back down letter by letter down to your balls. I love how are you're feeling inside and watch as you face lights up as the design begins. You seem captivated, almost not acknowledging me being there. But I know that if I stopped there would be hell to pay.

"Those birds on your neck have healed a treat mate," the tattooist smiles, dipping the needle in the black ink again.

"They look fucking perfect mate. I'm so pleased with them. And the boy likes them too! Don't ya boy?" you say, removing your eyes from the work in progress and looking at me.

"Yes Boss."

"Fuck Pitch, you have him well trained."

"I know. He knows what he has to do!"

You run your hand over your head and the feeling instantly comes back to me. I remember last time I shaved your head and sex that followed as a result. That day has been emblazoned on my brain and was the focus of many a wank session while I was away. But I'm back now and doing the business in hand.

"You like getting fucked don't you boy?"

"Yes," I say, moving myself a little faster on your meat. Lite me a cigarette and pass it to me!"

I light a cigarette, the smoke blown straight before I pass it to you. You take a deep lungful and blow the smoke back over me. Fuck it is so horny.

"Right, that's one done," the tattooist says, wiping the fresh artwork with tissue. "Do you want me to leave for a bit? I know you like to cum after every piece of work."

"No. Just get straight on with the other one."

I have to admit, I did feel a little cheated. I was expecting him to leave us so I could take your cum like we always do. But I consoled myself with the fact that at the end of this, there would be two new tats that would need my worshipping.

The tattooist moved around to the other side and you put the cigarette between your lips.

"How does it look?" you ask, holding up your fist before extending your middle finger.

"Perfect," I reply.

You open your hand and run it down my chest, over my nipple, down my belly towards my cock. You take another large drag and take out the cigarette from between your lips. You grab the back of my neck and pull me down and snog me. The tattooist looks up and smiles to himself. He dips the needle back into the ink and continues.

When you release my head and I sit back up, you have a contented smile on your face. You take another drag on your fag and look back down at the ink. I'm so excited, I return to fucking your hard inked cock with as much vigour as before.

"How much longer are you going to be?" you ask.

"Not that long. Nearly finished the outline, just need to colour in and that's you done."

"OK mate. Hold off a bit Nick, I don't wanna cum until he finished the last part!"

Slightly pissed off, I slow the fucking back down. You look down again watching the letters disappear and reappear and my hole works your dick. The image returns of fingering my hole when you came around earlier. Rediscovering the feeling and tightness that had only been missing for 2weeks.

"Right mate, we are nearly there. All I need to do is just a little bit of yellow and that's me done."

"OK. Nick, fuck my cock!" you bark.

Finally, this I what I had been waiting for. The cum drought for the last 2 weeks would finally soon be at an end. I move my hole harder and faster up and down your stiff shaft. Bam...Bam...Bam as my arse cheeks bang against your legs, my cunt almost aching for you to spurt.

"Yeah, that right your fucking little bastard. Take it. Harder!"

You look down at your hand.

"Almost there… last bit now Pitch," the tattooist says calmly.

"Oh yeah. Fuck! I'm gonna cum… I'm gonna fucking cum! CUUUUNT!"

Your cock explodes inside me. My body physically shakes as you blast thick white skinhead cum, which floods my insides. In return I shoot my load on your chest and belly as you pant, forcing out the last remaining sperm from your balls and cock inside me. I drop down onto you exhausted and your wrap you strong tattooed arms around me. At first I thought it was just an embrace but you held me firm.

"How about you inking 'Pitch's cunt' on his arse cheek?"

"What? No…"I gasped.

"Forget it. I'm not going anywhere near the business end mate!"

"None of my spunk will come out, I promise. I'll leave my cock inside him as a plug," you laugh.

"I really don't think…"

"Shut up," you snap, interrupting my protests.

"Alright mate. Seeing as it's you," The tattooist grins.

I Love Mornings

It's midsummer and the warm breeze is coming through the open window. You open your eyes and see me lying next to you, the flimsy sheet halfway down our bodies. As you look over, your cock overrides you brain and tells your body it needs action.

You slide the sheet down my body and spread my legs, getting your head down to lick my hole. Once satisfied, you slide your tongue over my balls and start sucking my cock. You look up to make sure I'm still asleep and you have nothing to worry about. Then you place your tattooed hands either side of me and lean over me on your locked inked arms. You're now hard cock is right against my hole. You push and your big fucking knob parts my cunt and your swallow disappears. Then as firmly as you dare, you push your inked shaft in, right up to your bulging bollocks. You begin to rock gently but firmly as your arse bobs between my legs, moving your stiff skinhead meat through my body.

You look down at my sleeping face and the fact that you are doing this without me knowing makes it even more exciting. You know bloody well that if I was awake and you wanted sex, I wouldn't have said no. I would have been only too grateful and accepted it in an instant whilst loving every minute of it. But I'm not and that added to the pleasure for you.

You lean down and gob on my nipple before, beginning to suck it. Your tongue flicks it before you grasp it firmly between your lips. I move, maybe my subconscious has been touched by your actions... but still I remain asleep. You release my nipple and bite my neck, clenching my skin in your teeth as you suck hard. You want to mark me, not only as a badge that I am your territory but to let everyone know that we have been fucking….again! When you release, you look down at me again. Your arse is pushing as hard as you dare so I won't wake up.

"Yeah, you gonna wake up with my little cunt inside you and you won't even fucking know!" you whisper, as your cock spurts your DNA deep inside me.

Your cock pumps, as thick white ropes of cum floods my body, before you roll off of me panting. As the panting subsides and your cock goes down to a semi. You light a cigarette as I blink my eyes open.

"Alright?" you ask.

"I'm not sure. It's too early to tell."

"You were knocking them back a bit last night!"

"Yeah. I need the loo," I say and walk over the en-suit.

You know that if I need a shit, I will find out you have just fucked me. But you smile to yourself as you hear me only pissing. I come out and click of the bathroom light before getting back onto the bed. My hand slides down your body and onto your cock.

"Did I fall over last night?"

"I don't know. Why?"

"I have a bruise on my neck."

"Oh yeah. So you have. Fuck knows how that happened!"

"Fuck me Pitch," I ask, kissing your neck

"OK… if you insist," you smile.

Close shave

Part 1

"Come on, get on with it. It's driving me fucking mad."

"I will," I shout.

"I haven't had my hair this long for years. I don't know why I fucking agreed to it."

"Because it's horny!" I call.

"Cunt," you say, softer but loud enough for me to hear.

I come back in the room and you're sitting stark bollock naked, except for your oxblood boots, with a cigarette hanging from your mouth. You place the packet down on the arm of the chair.

"Will you get a fucking move on?"

"OK. I'm ready."

I place the tray down on the small table next to the chair and work up lather.

"You had better do a fucking good job or you and me will have words!"

I sit on your lap. I have to admit, it was tempting… just to see what you would do to me. But I just smiled and started to lather your head.

"That feels fucking good. The itching is going already."

I can feel the beast between your legs begin to stir as I move the badger hair brush over your head. You take a large drag on your cigarette and blow it at me. I move your head to the side, partly to make sure I have the lather all over and partly to look at the freshly healed tat on your neck. First one side and then the other.

"Are you ready yet? I wanna get inside you!"

"Oh, I'm ready." I smiled.

I placed the lather pot and the brush down on the tray and lift myself up. I wanted to slide down your hard inked cock, to feel myself taking every inch you had to offer. But you had other ideas. BAM, straight in…no fucking messing. I gasp as my ring met your balls.

"Oh fuck, that feels good." I pick up the razor and begin running it over you scalp, leaving a track of clean smooth skin. "Fuck yeah. Get it all."

I rinse the razor in the jug of water and begin to scrape again. I can feel you cock twitching inside me… that was all I needed to know. I dipped the razor in the water again, my arse tightening and moving on your cock with my actions. I continue to shave with your solid cock lodged inside me.

"Fuck me as you do it. But don't cut me!" you snap, letting out a loud belch.

My cock twitches with delight and you glance down to check my response. You take the last drag on your cigarette before stubbing it out in the ashtray. Half your head is now clear and smooth and I put the razor down on the tray.

"Fuck Pitch. That's looking so fucking horny."

"Yeah? How does that neck look?"

"Perfect," I reply.

I lean forward and lick the swallow on the shaved side. I tingle as my tongue touches your warm skin and recalled riding you as you had it done.

"I have one on the other side you know!" you grin.

"I know. I will be getting to that when I have shaved that side."

I start to move with more purpose on your stiff cock. The image of your SKINHEAD tattoo down your shaft and the swallow on your knob is fixed in my mind.

You run your hands up my back and place them on my shoulders, restricting my movement but making the penetration so much deeper. Your muscles flexing as you push down.

"Fuck Nick, you dirty little fucker. That's so good."

"Fuck me. Fuck me harder."

"Oh I will… after you have finished my head. Until then, you have to do all the work. Think of it as…."

"An incentive?"

"I was going to say punishment but yeah, incentive will do."

You release your grip allowing me to increase the motion once more. I can hear your boots creaking with every movement. You wrap your boot around the leg of another small table and pull it towards us and place your leg up on it. I reach back and run my fingers up it, reaching down as far as I can then run it back up your laces pulled tight around your leg.

"That should be your tongue!"

"I know. It will be soon enough."

"It had better be you bastard."

I push you back on the chair and lick you nipples. You raise your arm and I run my tongue over to your armpit. You push me back and flem on my chest.

"Pitch, I'm getting fucking close."

"No! Don't cum! I always cum first, you fucking know that."

I clench my arse muscles and you close your eyes.

"FUCKING CUNT. That's not fair."

"Come on Pitch, Cum inside me. Fill me up with you skinhead cum mate."

"You fucking want it?"

"Yes mate, do it for me."

"Beg me!"

"Please Pitch. Please cum for me Boss. Give me your DNA… I need you to fill me… PLEASE!"

"Fuck…fuck… YOU FUCKING CUNT!" you bellow.

You drop your leg back down onto the floor and push as hard as you can. Your cock is so deep it feels like it's gonna come out of my mouth. Your dick pulses, pumping thick wave after wave of skinhead seamen into my insides. Finally, there is nothing to stop me and I blast my cum over your chest and belly. We both pant, eager to catch our breath.

"Now…can you… finish... my fucking head?"

"Sure," I smile, "...just leave the beast exactly where he is!"

Part 2

You sit forward. I grab the towel and wipe the shaving foam from the back of the chair and from the shaven half of your head. You grab your cigarettes and light another one, savouring it.

"I love smoking after sex."

"I love you smoking during and after sex," I laugh.

I turn your head and look again at the swallow tattoo on this side.

"Not until you have sorted out this side you fucker," you pant, taking a drag on your cigarette and not even looking at me.

I pick up the razor again. I can hear the scraping as the razor clears the hair from your head, leaving a smooth clear line.

"That's feeling better already. I can't wait until you get that shit off my head."

I rinse the razor and you begin to smile.

"What?"

"I can feel my cum running down my balls," you laugh.

I reach around and run my thumb over your balls, scooping up your spillage before sucking it off.

"That's that sorted," I laugh.

I clear the side of your head and you lean forward so I can do the back. You rest you head on my chest so I can reach the top of your neck and shave the back of your head. You pass the time spitting on me and watching it trickle down and drip of my cock.

"Sit back," I said.

"What about this strip in the middle. It's a fucking Mohican."

"I like it. I might leave it!" I laugh.

You clench your fist.

"Get... it... fucking... off!"

"OK, OK." I smile.

I rinse the razor again and scrape the remaining strip from your scalp. You grab a clean towel and wipe the remaining suds from your head. You put the cigarette back between your lips and run your hands over your smooth scalp before leaning your head back, resting it on the palms of your hands.

"Come on Nick, get off for a minute."

"What? Why?"

"I need to go for a piss." I raise my eyebrows and grin broadly. "Fuck me; you are a real dirty fucking cunt aren't ya?" I say nothing. "OK!"

I move my hole up and down your cock slowly before stopping. You start to empty your bladder and I start to feel the hot liquid surround your cock inside me. I fucking love the feeling but you just raise your middle finger before replacing you hand back beneath your head. Once finished, you take the cigarette end out of your mouth.

"Right, now you have to get up. I need to clean up a bit."

Reluctantly, I get up and have to run the toilet to empty your piss. You stand up and grab the towel, rubbing your still hard cock and balls.

"Don't worry, It's not over yet!" you shout.

You walk over to the fridge and take out a can of lager. You pull the ring and foam drips down onto you cock before you take a large swig. I come back from the bathroom and you walk back to the lounge.

"Get down on the fucking floor."

"Give us a towel to lie on," I ask.

"Don't be a pussy and get on the fucking floor."

I lay down on the laminate floor and you kick my legs apart with your 14 hole oxblood boot. You put the sole of your boot on my now semi cock and begin to rub it. I look up at your still hard cock and my cock gets harder beneath your boot. You take your weight on your hands, locking your arms as you ram you hard cock inside me again.

"Mmm fuck," you almost whisper.

You pick up your can and drain the remaining lager from it, before throwing the can to one side. You begin to fuck, stabbing your arse down and ramming your still solid meat inside me. I grip your tattooed arms and bend my legs a little to give you easier access. You let out a large lager smelling belch as you continue to fuck me. It fucking drives me wild.

"Now that's a proper fucking burp from a proper skin bloke!"

"Fuck Pitch."

"I know what you want but not yet, you cunt. I want you to want it!"

"I want it mate. I fucking want it."

"Not yet. We got plenty of fucking to do yet, ya fucking little bastard. You're getting fucked by this proper skinhead cunt!" I run my hands down your back and onto your arse, pounding between my legs. My body moved with every thrust you make and I'm fucking loving it. "Rub my fucking head!"

I place my hand on your scalp and run my fingers over your smooth skin. I feel your cock stiffen even harder inside me as my fingers glide over your flesh. Suddenly, you stop fucking and look down at me panting.

"OK. That wasn't the reaction I was expecting," I said.

"I want another fag!"

You withdraw your cock and walk over to your packet, still sitting on arm of the chair, your cock still standing to attention. You light another cigarette, pick up the ashtray and come back down between my legs, pushing back into me. You prop yourself up on you forearms and blow smoke rings into my face. I cough but you just laugh.

"Don't fucking give me that! You fucking love it. You know you do. Having sex and getting used by a smoking, belching, tattooed skinhead cunt like me."

"You know I do."

"I don't know what I'm going to get tattooed next…my hands…my chest….maybe even my bollocks." I move my arse beneath you but you refuse to thrust. "I've had my cock and knob done… well you know, you've got them buried inside you at the moment. So I might get my balls done and have a full fucking set." Fuck this is so frustrating. Everything you're saying is turning me on so fucking much. And you know it! You let out another loud, long, larger burp, before you take another drag on your cigarette.

Finally you relent and slam your arse down hard, forcing your cock to stab inside me.

"Argh, fuck!" I say, through gritted teeth.

"I've only just started," you smile. You place the cigarette in the ashtray and really start to pummel my hole. I thought your strokes were hard before but now you are really raping my cunt. The smell of man sex hung heavy in the air as the moaning and heavy breathing intensified. You throw your head back and arch your back, driving your cock deeper as you blast another load of fertility into me. As you arse stabs your cock to release its load, you rip a loud fart, causing me to almost convulse beneath you. You drop down on top of me, your full weight bearing down as you continue to fart. As the air turns rancid I can hold back no longer. My cock spurt cum and our skin begins to stick together.

Part 3

We lay panting for a while before you roll off of me. You wipe the sweat from your face with your hand before running it over your smooth bonehead.

"Fuck me. That was good", I panted, gasping for breath.

"I'm going to," you smile "… one last time. For now anyway."

You stand up and pull me to my feet. You grab me by the back of my neck and march me over the sideboard in front of the mirror. You push me forward and I lay my head on my hands as you push back into me. You look at your reflection.

"You're lucky you did a good job on my head," you snarl. "Now, you do all the work." You stand there behind me, staring at yourself. I begin to rock backwards and forwards in front of you. "You remember the sex after the punch ups I had? Of course you do, you fucking loved it. That bastard in the pub… bam... bam... smack," you say, jabbing your arms in the mirror. "And that cunt in street? Yeah, dragged him into that alley and almost killed the cunt…. Bam... bam... bam," you smile as your arms relive their glory. "My fucking boots got a look in too. These boots, which have been fucking you in all morning. Yeah, this big skinhead cunt doesn't stand for no shit or disrespect." The images flashed back into my mind. Your heavy blows knocking him to the ground then your boots kicking and stamping him… so fucking horny. "And then I bang you right there in the alley. Bleachers down and my cock shagging the shit out of your arse. Can you feel those cold wet bricks against your face nick?"

"Yeah, I can feel them," was all I could manage.

The noise of the city going on around us with the creaking of my boots, just being heard, as you fuck me.

I smile to myself and groan with pleasure. I'm pushing back on your cock, impaling myself as your crutch slams against my arse cheeks. I hate this position because I can't see what's happening. But it feels so good.

"I remember."

"Yeah of course you do. You got to see me in action that night. I'm sure I felt that bastard's jaw break!" You grip my hips and now you start to fuck too. "I'm getting close. I'm gonna spill again, right up your fucked, cum soaked cunt," you growl.

You nearly push me through the sideboard as you empty your balls inside me again. Your cock pulses as it oozes another load of batter inside me. You open a drawer and take out a butt plug. You slowly pull out your cock before quickly pushing the plug inside me.

"That should keep my DNA inside you. Now get dressed, we're going to the pub!" you smile, smacking my arse.

Cruisin Fer a Bruisin

Part One

We are in a mixed pub we sometimes go to for a change. We are standing to the side just drinking our beers and keeping ourselves to ourselves. You are getting a lot of looks and love the attention and I'm just happy to been seen with you. There is a group of 4 people standing close to us, with one bloke shouting his mouth off, loving the sound of his own voice.

"The problem with the skin scene nowadays is all the queers. Fucking gays thinking it's cool to look like a skinhead. Makes me fucking sick."

Your eye stay fixed on him and I can see the rage beginning to build inside you. But you say nothing and bide your time.

***

After about an hour three of the group say their goodbyes, leaving the mouthy fucker alone in the pub. The man finishes his drink and begins to make his way to the toilets.

"Hold this," you say, passing me your half empty glass. "And don't put it down or some cunt will drink it!" you say and make your way down to the toilets.

"Fuck off," I whisper. "I'm not missing this."

***

I walk downstairs to the toilets and stand in the doorway. You already have the bloke by the trough, giving him a piece of your mind.

"You got a thing against gays? You fucking cunt. You wanna fucking say it to my face, you fucking narrow minded little shit?"

"No I, I didn't mean…."

"Oh yes you did mean…" you snarl, punching him in the guts.

He doubles over in pain but you push him back upright, punching him in the face and breaking his nose. Two more punches and his jaw shatters beneath his skin before you punch him in the stomach again and he drops to his knees. Your boot comes up and kicks him in his already battered and bleeding face. He goes down like a sack of shit but you keep kicking him in the stomach.

"Cunt! You fucking narrow minded cunt!" You look over at me, rage boiling in your eyes. "Put them drinks down and get your fucking arse over here now!"

I place the drinks down on a shelf above the sinks and come over as quickly as I could. Your cock is standing hard and to attention between your open bleachers, held up by your white braces. You undo my bleachers and spin me around.

"You hate gays do you, you piece of shit? Well you're going to watch me fuck him!"

The man is lying on his back with your boot holding him down on his chest. You ram your hard tattooed cock full length inside me. You fuck hard, removing you braces from your shoulder and letting them hang as you take off your shirt. You lay it on a sink next to you and replace you braces over your bare shoulders. You look down at my 'Pitch's Cunt' tattoo on my arse and watch your inked cock ploughing in and out of my tight fuck hole…. Skin… gone…. Skinh…. gone….. skinhea… gone. You look down and gob on the blooded face of the man beneath your boot.

"Are you watching? You piece of shit?" you snarl, and stamp on his chest again.

You look at my face in the mirror, grimacing as you screw my hole. Your gaze turns to your body, admiring your ink with every motion of your body. You look beyond yourself, to the reflection in the mirror behind you, watching the Skinhead tattoo across your shoulders and your firm arse cheeks as they ram your skinhead meat inside me.

"Are you ready, you cunt?" you say to me. "Are you ready you worthless bastard?" you say to body in pain beneath your boot.

You push hard inside me, exaggerating your breathing as your cock fires thick white jets of cum into me. I gasp as I feel your rock hard meat pumping every last drop into me. You pull out of me and your cock is still hard as fuck.

"You... go back up stairs and take the drinks. Once we down them we are fucking leaving!" I pull up my bleachers and grab the drinks, staggering back to the doorway. "And you, you sack of fucking shit. Don't you ever let me see you again. Understand?"

The battered body nods then doubles over again as you give him one last kick to remember you by.

Part Two

Outside the night air is chilly. But you hand me your shirt and look around.

"Taxi," you shout but it passes us by. "No matter, we'll fucking walk!"

All the way back to my house, your stamping your boots on the pavement as you walk, as the anger still raged inside you. You shout "what the fuck are you looking at?" to anyone who walked passed, if they were looking at us or not.

***

Once back at mine, I breathed a sigh of relief that at least no one else was going to get their head kicked in (no matter how much I loved watching you fight.) But then, I held my breath as I knew all the frustration inside you was now going to be taken out on me. Once inside, I place your shirt down on the table in the hall as you walk straight into the lounge.

"Nick! Get your fucked arse in here now!"

I walk into the doorway as you undo your bleachers.

"Did you hear him? Did you fucking hear that fucking cunt?"

"Yeah."

"I fucking showed him. Bastard!"

"Pitch, I just need the toilet."

"What? Right. Don't be fucking long!"

"Yeah, OK."

***

I walk out of the lounge and upstairs to the bathroom. I lean on the sink and take deep breaths. I haven't seen you that worked up for a long time and although it is fucking horny… it is scary. I play the events again in my mind, the punches, the kicks … I really thought you were going to kill him. Then… the sex. It was so intense. Almost primal. Watching you admiring yourself, as you fucked, still dishing out pain to the snivelling wretch under your boot.

"Nick!"

I flush the chain and go back downstairs.

***

As I enter the lounge you are naked. You're sitting on the settee, just finishing tying the laces on your 14 hole boots. You light a cigarette and take a large lungful.

"Don't stand in door. Get over here and suck my fucking cock! No… I'm too wound up for all that shit now. I just wanna fuck!"

As I start to strip, you stand up and walk over the fireplace. You touch your cigarette onto the newspaper in the fireplace and in no time, the wood is crackling as the flames roared. Now naked, you beckon me over and I walk across the room. You place your hand on my shoulder and push me down so I'm lying on the sheepskin rug in front of the fire. Images of John flashed back into my mind, from years ago. You push my legs apart and lean over me, your strong tattooed arms locked straight as you look down into my eyes. Your face hardly changes as you push into me. Your thrusts are hard and purposeful straight from the off, our bodies kissed by the warmth of the fire. I move with every movement your body makes.

"I showed him. That fucking wanker! He's not fucking mouthing off now is he?"

"No," I manage to say between gasps.

"That fucking piece of shit! That will teach him to fuck around with me!"

"Yes," I gasp.

"I fucking taught him a thing or two when I fucked you as well. Didn't I?"

"Yes. Fuck Pitch, that so good."

"Yeah, you love my fucking hard inked cock up your guts. Getting fucked by a real fucking man, not an arsehole like that!"

You push as your cock spurts another big load inside me. You grit your teeth as you pump, emptying your balls inside me. Before continuing to fuck.

"Thinks he can fucking piss me off? Nobody pisses me off. Do they?"

"No Pitch," I gasp.

"Tell me, you little cunt! Tell me what I am!"

"You're a real skinhead man. You are my Boss."

"Yeah, that's what I like to fucking hear. I demand respect. And when I don't get it, I'll fuck any bastard over."

Your words mixed with another arse full of cum and the continued hard merciless sex, is driving me mad. I reach up and run my fingers up your belly and onto your chest. As I touch your nipples your cock twitches inside me, making you fuck harder. I run my fingers down your sweat soaked back and onto your pounding arse. Your thrusts are getting harder and more ferocious. It feels like my pelvis would break at any moment.

"Pitch, I'm…"

But I could not complete the sentence, before I shoot a thick white mess up my belly.

"I'm fucking cumin," you bellow and your body convulses, as you dump another load of sperm inside me.

You drop down on top of me, panting heavily, before you lift yourself up onto your forearms and flick your cigarette butt into the fire. You take out another cigarette and light it.

"Twice… back to back. I'm proud of myself."

"Me too. Feel better?"

"About cumming three times in less than twenty minutes? Yeah! Not about the fucking wanker though. Fucking winds me up," you say, taking a large drag on your fag and blowing it over me. I struggle and cough but I'm pinned beneath your body and skewered by your still hard shaft. I'm going nowhere. "Did you fucking see the state of him when I had finished?"

"Yeah. What a fucking mess."

"Too right. I hope I fucking crippled the wanker. See all that blood? Fuck, what a mess. I did that, with these..," you say, making a fist, "…and my fucking boots. I know he will have a boot mark on his boat-race for fucking weeks," you laugh. "Still, you love seeing me fight. So it's all good. I get to teach some cunt a lesson and you get your jollies and a shag afterwards."

"Yeah, about that. Pitch, I have a confession to make."

"What the fuck have you done? You little cunt."

"You remember the bloke that you dragged into the alley and kicked the crap out of?"

"The one that called me a wanker? Yeah?"

"Well… I paid him to take a beating."

"You what?"

"I paid him. I love seeing you fight and the sex after is fantastic….so, I made sure it happened."

"What about that fuckwit tonight?"

"Never seen him before in my life!"

"Well next time, tell me. After I have beaten the shit out of him and fucked you, I will rob the cunt. I might as well make it worth my while. It will pay for some more ink at least."

"You prostitute!" I laugh; relieved I am not going to get a beating.

"No mate, the sex is free… it's the fighting you'll be paying for. You little fucker!" you smile, taking another drag of your fag. "Nick, can I ask you a question?"

"What mate?"

"Can I move… my arse is getting fucking hot," you laugh. You roll off, away from the fire, throwing you cigarette end in the flames. I look over at you, basking in the afterglow of sex. "Oi, I said my arse was hot, I didn't say anything about being finished. Get this fucking cock back in your cum soaked arse! You have a lot of making up to do yet, ya scheming little fucker." I straddle you as some cum runs out of me and drops on your belly. "You dirty fucker. Your cunt is leaking." You scoop it up in your fingers and run it over your cock. "Now, get the beast back in there and fuck this skinhead bastard!" I push myself back onto you, my hole only too willing to welcome you back inside me. "That's it you bastard, take my tool. Fuck me!"

I begin to fuck you again and you place your hands under you smooth shaven head. "Come on Nick, this isn't a fucking children's ride. We are supposed to be fucking. FUCK ME!" I pick up the pace and a satisfied smirk creeps across your face. "You know, I have a belly full of beer don't ya. I can't make any promises about what's going to happen. Actually, I can!" you laugh.

You roar a loud burp which makes me fuck you harder. My cock spurts over your belly and chest but I don't stop. You feel your spunk begin to rise. You raise your booted leg and as you cock pumps another thick load inside me, you release a mighty fart. You sniff and begin to laugh.

"Shit that fucking stinks."

Part Three

You drop another couple of farts and I look down at you, panting hard.

"Fucking hell," I pant.

"You're not done yet, ya little cunt."

"What?"

"Get down and shine my fucking knob!"

I reluctantly climb off of you and your cock thuds down onto your belly. I lay down in 69 position and I take you into my mouth. Fuck you taste so good. I can taste my cunt and your sperm still clinging to your shaft. I can taste your ink, your dominance and your aggression. But most of all, I can taste the skinhead God that defines you. You take a cigarette out of the packet and light it. A small stream of spunk begins to run out of my hole. You lift up my leg and lean over, licking it up with your tongue, before lowering my leg again. You push your middle finger into me and I grunt with your cock still inside my mouth.

"MMM those little bastards have to be recycled and with my finger in there, it should stop any more escapees. Don't worry you'll be getting them back soon enough."

You rest your head on my leg and blow smoke over the tattoo on my arse cheek before rubbing your smooth shaved head over my thigh. You lower your hand and push my head deeper down onto your shaft.

"That's right boy, get that fucking swallow right fucking down your throat. See if you can suck the ink right out of my bell end and shaft." Your words turn me on so much but just in case there was any doubt, you rip another fart out. Your cock vibrates down my tight hot throat, increasing the pleasure for both of us. "Yeah, that's right. You fucking love sucking this skinhead's cock don't you boy? You love getting skull fucked."

The heat from the fire is burning against my back but I have intention of moving. I'm lost in the moment, savouring your taste and listening to your words. You finish the cigarette and throw the glowing end into the flames again.

You roll over, pushing me onto my back. Now you're free for your arse to push your hard fucking tool even deeper. Your balls flop down blocking my nose and I gag as I can't breathe and my eyes start to water. I feel like I could suffocate but even if I did I know I would die happy. Through gritted teeth you unleash another heavy load of spunk from the beast.

"That's it, swallow my little fucking skins, you cunt!"

I frantically swallow, desperate not to choke any more than I already am. You roll off of me panting as air rushes back into my lungs.

***

I get up and go to the kitchen for a beer. The light from the fridge door illuminated the kitchen. My hole is sore from all the punishment it has received. I run my hand under the cold tap and try to sooth my ring but when I place it back under the tap again, blood mixes with the water.

"Fuck... he has broken me," I whisper.

***

I kicked the fridge door closed went back into the lounge, complete with two cans of ice cold lager, only to find you lying on the rug asleep. I put one can down on the table and open the other, taking a large mouthful.

"I wonder?" I ask myself.

I put the can down on the floor, knelt down and started to wank your flaccid cock which sparks back into life as the beast begins to wake from his slumber. The ink from the swallow looked so bright and clear, wet from the vast amount of cum it had expelled. I opened my hand and gripped the side of your cock with my thumb and first finger. I hate doing it like this but it allows me to watch as the letters expand on your shaft.

In no time the beast is full awake and raring to get back into action. I walk over to the drawers and take out a pair of handcuffs. I clip one to your wrist, feed it around the leg of the heavy coffee table and clip the other end to your other arm. I straddle you again and rub your swallow on my sore, fucked arse. I lower myself onto you and you, move gently as your sleep between my legs. It feels like I'm standing on a narrow rim between excruciating pain and total ecstasy. I have to bite my finger to stop myself crying out as I start to fuck you harder. You move in your sleep, raising your arm up to your face.

I close my eyes and all I can imagine is your inked tool, all I feel is your solid tool inside me. But then you wake up.

"And what the fuck do you think you're doing? You fucking little cunt! Let me out of this! Was that session not enough for you? Not enough that you need to fuck me in my sleep? When I get out of here you're gonna get it … and no more Mr Nice Guy!"

I ignore you. I close my eyes and savour the feeling of your thick meat inside me. I move my body faster and harder. I cry out in pain but your just look up at me, bellowing "shut the fuck up… you wanted it, fucking take it, you little bitch!"

You gob again onto my chest but I'm moving so violently it doesn't stay there long. It ran down my chest and the full length of my body before dripping off my cock and onto your belly. You arch your back and ram your dick as deep as you can. You cock erupts, forcing another smaller load deep inside me. At the same time I pump my cum up my belly. Panting heavily, I drop down onto your body.

"OK Nick… you have got what you wanted. Now let me up."

I stand up and look down at you.

"I'm going to bed… and you're staying here. And I will decide when I want it again, understood?" I said, leaving before I get a reply.

Sex Alley

It's late. It's just stopped raining and we have left the club... half pissed. I can't wait to get home, we need to fuck. We run down the road, kicking car doors and filling the air with the sound of car alarms. You pick up a wheelie bin and throw it through a shop window before running off down the road. A passer-by starts chasing us but we run down an alley and hide behind some bins. The man stops by us and looks around. You run out and start punching and kicking him. Blood starts to run down his face as he drops to the ground. You stamp on his face and kick him in the guts, just for good measure.

"You wanna be a hero do you? You fucking cunt!"

You kick him again and gob on his face.

"Nick, I got blood on my boots. Fucking clean it off."

I drop to my knees and begin to lick your boots. My tongue slides over your smooth black boots, then up your leg before beginning their descent back down.

"Mmmm. Make sure they are fucking clean, I don't want any of that piece of shit left on my boots.

The taste of blood is heavy in my mouth. I hate the taste but that is over taken but the knowledge of the damage that these boots have inflicted. And not just tonight. You gob which hits the side of my face. You smile with delight as you watch it run down my face and drip onto your boot. The smile broadens when my tongue spreads it around your glossy black boot. You reach down and grab my jacket, pulling me back to my feet. You snog me hard and we rub each others smooth shaved heads.

"I have a surprise for you mate!" you say, opening up your jacket and taking out a glass.

"What the fuck?"

"I nicked it from the club but that's not all." Also from inside your jacket you bring out a bottle of vodka. "Nicked that fucker too!" I smiled as I knew that was coming. You pulled the optic off of the end of the bottle and tipped some vodka into the bottom of the glass. "Fill the rest up!" you bark.

I pull my cock out and piss into the glass, filling it to top. But I'm not finished, and as you take a large mouthful, I finish by pissing over your boots that I have just cleaned and the man lying unconscious on the ground.

You put the glass down on a bin and push me against the wall, opening my bleachers as your tongue and finger works my hole. It feels so fucking good mate, bet it tastes sweet as fuck! The noise of the city is carrying on around us as you take off my jacket. You pull my Fred Perry polo shirt over my head and yank my bleachers down even further to explore my body, ready for your own gratification. You stand up and kick my legs apart, spreading them as you push your hard cock inside me. I can feel you pressing against my back and the metal cock ring against my hole. I cry out in a mixture of pain and pleasure. 'No fucking use for lube as that's for wimps!' I hear in my head, as you have said it so frequently. The only problem is, I can't see you as you drive your cock in and out of my fucking tight cunt, as my face is pressed against cold wet brickwork. But it feels fucking amazing and my imagination is working overtime. Despite the noises of the traffic, I can hear you breathing as you push your cock in and out of my hole.

"You're fucking loving that, aren't you? You dirty fucking bitch!"

"Oh fuck yeah Pitch, fuck my cunt!"

"You don't have a cunt… its mine! Mine to fuck, mine to breed and mine to do whatever I fucking want with!"

I can hear you fumbling in your pocket. My heart almost misses a beat. What is coming now? Oh fuck, what is he doing? Then I hear a familiar click... it's a lighter. I place my hands against the cold wet brickwork and push myself back onto your hard meat, as you blow smoke, is carried away on slight breeze. Your hard shaft is driving me harder; your full, heavy, low hanging bollocks smacking against me.

"Is that deep enough in your arse, you bastard?"

"Oh fuck yeah. I fucking love it Pitch."

"Yeah Nick. I'm gonna fuck my little bastard into your cunt mate. Is that what you want?"

"Yes. Fuck yes."

Then, without warning, your cock erupts inside me. But it's not cum... It's hot wet piss, filling my insides. Then, once your bladder is empty, you start fucking me again.

"Are you ready to mix cum with that piss mate?"

I can't hold back any longer.

"Pitch, I'm going to cum mate."

"Yeah, do it Nick you fucking bastard. Cum while you're getting fucked by this fucking skinhead cunt!"

But you don't take you cock out of me. You simply pull me back against you as my cock spurts reams of this white cum down onto your 30 hole boots. Your arse is fucking pounding now. Your cock seems to stiffen harder as you fuck your piss inside me. Then your cock pumps thick white jets of cum inside my guts. You cry out as you ram hard, getting that cum as deep inside me as you can. Fuck I wish I could see you cumming...but its feels amazing!

You lean against me panting as your cock spits your last few kids into my cunt. You pull out of me, your hard cock still standing proud between your legs as you start to walk home, doing up your bleachers and leaving me used and full in the alley.

"Bring that fucking glass with you!" you call, as you disappear into the night.

I pull up my bleachers just as the bloke on the ground starts to come around.

"What…. What the fuck happened?"

"Mate… you don't know what you missed!" I smile, before kicking him in the face again and following you into the darkness.

Leather Night

The night is just right…not too hot so you sweat your tits off and not too cold so you freeze your bollocks off… just right to be covered in leather. The curtain moved gently in the breeze from the open window as we stand close to each other. I fucking love seeing you in full leather… from the cap on your head, the jacket wrapped around your body, the gloves covering your hands, the leather trousers hugging your strong legs, down to those horny boots I love. I raise my hands and run my fingers over your leather jacket, sliding them down to unfasten the button on your trousers. My mind flashes back to my childhood. The feeling of anticipation, unwrapping presents at birthdays and Christmas. That feeling returned before Pop…and it's open.

You take out a cigar from your pocket and light it as I watch. My fingers grasp the zip of your flies and slowly begin to pull it down…bit by bit… not enough to allow them to fall, just enough to gain access. With the cigar clamped in your mouth, your gloved hands are free to work on my body. I'm naked… nothing on to hide behind, exposed, just for you. One hand clasps my nipple while the other takes the cigar out from your mouth, then cups the back of my smoothly shaven head. You pull my face towards you, my lips stopping centimetres from yours. Your lips part and blow a steady stream of smoke at mine. I breathe in your smoke, turned on by the fact that the smoke is not only yours but has been down inside your body, before entering mine. I slide my hand down inside your leather trousers…. the beast is asleep! I wrap my fingers around your flaccid dick and begin to coax him awake. I run my finger along your shaft to the head of your cock, which twitches in response. Then I run my fingers back down to feel your leather cock ring nestling in your pubes. Now that makes my cock twitch!

I pull your trousers down and your now semi hard cock springs from its cage. The beast is very much awake! You can feel my warm breath touch your skin as my tongue slides up the full length of your shaft… up and up, right to the top... then down your hard cock and over your bulging balls. Fuck you taste so fucking good. I open my mouth and take you inside. My lips close around your shaft as they slide back down your meat until they touch your balls again. The scent of the leather is heavy in my nostrils as your cock lodges in my throat. I choke, my eyes watering as I gag, before I slide back up your shaft. My tongue flicks the swallow on your knob and it pulses with delight before I start to work my way back down towards your heavy, low hanging balls. As my head bobs between your legs, you take a large lungful of smoke. As you exhale, it curls around me, making me work even harder. I savour the taste of you, the smell from the cigar smoke and leather still covering your body.

Fuck mate, I can't hold this back any longer... I need to feel you inside me! I straddle you and your knob rubs against my tight fuck hole. I ease down just as you take another drag on your cigar...fuck, you're in. I unzip your jacket and pull it apart, revealing the black leather harness criss-crossing your body. I physically gasp mate...you look amazing. Finally, the present underneath all that wrapping! I slide my hole down your tool, deeper and deeper as I take it inside me. Fuck, it feels so good! You take another large lungful of smoke and I watch you exhale. My fingers rub your skin between the leather straps, accidentally touching your nipple. Your cock twitches deep inside me...now I know you're secret.

I move my hole faster and harder up and down your hard cock, our bodies glistening with sweat. I cry out in a mixture of pain and pleasure as you relight the cigar. I'm fucking you harder and faster still… almost raping your fucking hard shaft.

"Yes boy. Fuck me! FUCK ME!" you say, as your cock slices through my body.

I can't hold back any more. I close my eyes as I spurt my cum up your belly and chest.

"Fuck yeah," you grin. "You want me to do that? You want Pitch to cum in your fucking cunt boy? Do ya? Oh fuck. I'm gonna cum...I'm gonna fucking cum," you shout, as your cock explodes deep inside me. I can feel your cock pulsing as you pump your thick white cum inside me.

I lean against you, drained as we both pant hard. You take another large lungful of smoke before panting, "Round two?"

No Hope

"So, what do you want done?" you ask.

"Well look at it! The paint is tired, there are lumps out of the plaster and it stained with nicotine because you smoke!"

"True. But it's usually during or after sex! And I'm sure you don't want me to stop that!"

"No! Fuck no!" I chuckled.

"OK. Well if we are going to do this, I suppose we had better get started!"

I go into the kitchen, open the fridge and return with two can of larger. You're bent over, working on the paint tin lid with a screwdriver. I stand and watch for a moment. I know what is under that old, hole studded Union Jack t-shirt and ripped bleachers. Fuck, it is such a shame that it's obscured by clothes. My eyes fix on the tattoos on your bare arms and I stand transfixed.

"What the fuck are you doing, brewing the fucking larger?"

"Sorry," I say, snapping back to reality. "I was just watching a master at work!" I say, passing you a can.

"You're fucking right I am… and don't you forget it! Well, open it then! I can't do fucking everything!"

"Er, of course. Sorry!"

The paint tin lid pops off and you take a large mouthful of larger.

"Fuck that's good!"

The sun is hot outside, making the temperature sore in the lounge. The windows are open and a breeze is coming through the open back door… but it's warm air.

"Right, I'll have the roller and you use the paint brush. I don't think you can be fucking trusted with a roller. You useless cunt!"

"Sure, thanks."

I didn't know why I was thanking Pitch but it just seemed the right thing to say. You run the roller in the tray and run it up and down on the wall.

"Yeah, I think this will look fucking amazing by the time we finish."

"I hope so."

"Have faith little man," you smile.

Fuck, I love watching you. Even something stupid and mundane like painting, seems to take on a different presence when it's you. My mind begins to race and plans starts forming.

"Of course, you know we really should be doing this naked. I mean, we could get covered in paint!"

"That's why we have old clothes on!" you say, sarcastically.

"Yeah, I know, but…."

You stop and look at me, watching me squirm to justify what I have just said.

"What?" you ask blankly.

"Well, we are only going to get fucking hot mate aren't we? I mean, clothes can be so restrictive."

"You just wanna fucking see my body, ya dirty little fucker."

"Well, that's not a bad thing!" I smile, embarrassed.

"Well you only had to fucking say. No need to make up fucking excuses."

You put the paint tray and roller down and peel off the battered old t-shirt. My eyes follow the frayed bottom of the t-shirt skimming up your belly, over your nipples, up your chest and over your head. Fuck… my knees are going fucking weak. Your hands unbuckle the button on your ripped bleachers.

"Well… this isn't a floor show. Fucking strip!" You bark.

"Of course."

I pull my polo shirt over my head and drop my jeans, standing naked in no time.

"Fucking hell, that wasn't planned at all was it? You have no hope of getting this done if you keep initiating sex!"

I did not reply. I just watched as your ripped bleachers dropped to the floor, quickly followed by your boxers. You pick up your can and take another large mouthful of larger. I want you to grab me by the back of my head and pull me over to you, forcing me onto my knees to take your pierced, inked cock into my mouth…but you don't. You just pick up the tray and roller and carry on. Damn!

I pick up the brush and start painting again. You look at me, watching me paint and smile to yourself. You know what I want and know how much I want. But you are just being a bastard. Well, for now anyway! I move across in front of you and place my can of beer down on the floor. I try a new tactic of seduction… full bloody blatant encouragement. I paint next to you and I can see out of the corner of my eye that you are looking me up and down. You put the tray of paint down on top of a wooden stool. You continue rolling while your other hand slaps my arse cheeks really hard.

"Fuck," I shout.

"That wasn't hard. This is hard!"

Wham! Your hand slaps me again.

"Fucking hell!"

"Wimp," you chuckle.

You run the roller in the paint in the tray while your other hand rubs my now red arse cheek. I close my eyes and spread my legs slightly. You take the opportunity and push your middle finger into my tight hole.

"Fuck that's good," you smile.

You move your finger in and out of my fuck hole, slowly at first then moving faster and harder. Paint is the furthest thing from my mind as I lean against the wall, gasping as your finger moves.

"Fuck yeah… fuck yeah…. Fuck, fuck, FUCK," I cry.

You pull your finger out and drain your can.

"Get me another one," you ask.

"Here, have mine."

You take my can smiling.

"Now get on your fucking knees!"

I kneel down on the carpet as you begin to paint again, roller in one hand and the can in the other. My tongue touches the end of your knob. I can feel the metal and taste your knob as my tongue begins to move around the head of your cock. It glides over the swallow tattoo, around the side, over the pa and back up. The beast begins to stir, waking from his slumber. I run my tongue down the underside of your cock, down your shaft and onto your balls. I can feel your body moving as I am under you, my tongue massaging your bollocks and my eyes looking at the crack of your arse. I come back up your rod, moving my tongue up the base of your dick and back along the top… my saliva glistening from the light of the window, bringing to life the letters on your cock….S… K…I…N…H…E…A…D… then back to the swallow on your knob.

Your cock is now semi hard. I open my mouth and take you inside me, it tastes so fucking good. Although my eyes are closed, I can feel your body turn to run the roller in the paint then turn back to face the wall, as your other hand brings the can back up to your lips then back down.

"You fucking little cunt. That feels so fucking nice. You love having this skinhead bastard in your mouth, don't you boy!" I said nothing. I wanted to shout 'yes'. I wanted to tell you that I wanted you inside me, I wanted to feel your cock, ripping through my body as you fucked me hard. But that would mean taking your tool out of my mouth and I'm not that stupid! So I said nothing. "Yeah, of course you fucking do!" you continued.

I feel like I'm in heaven. The heat of the room is intensifying as the warm breeze caresses our bodies, making the hairs on my body stand on end and sending a shiver down my body. I place my hand on your arse and you start to move, very slowly fucking my face. I place my hands on your hips and hold my head still as your pelvis rocks backwards and forwards. You put the can down and place your hand on the back of my shaved head. I feel your body turn again and roll the roller in the paint tray before continuing to roll it on the wall.

"Fuck that feel so fucking good in your hot little mouth. I would love to have you suck me while I do the whole room."

I take your cock out of my mouth.

"I don't think so…" I pant, "…you have to fuck me!"

"I fucking knew you would say that! Get up and light me a fag!"

I stand up and take your cigarettes out of your jacket pocket, hanging over a chair. I light it and pass it to you. You take a large lungful of smoke and look around.

"So how much do you think we will be doing today?" you ask.

"Well if we carry on like this, not a lot," I joked. "I would like to get up to there…" I point, forgetting I still have the paint brush in my hand.

Paint splatters across your belly… fuck, what have I done?

"Bastard" you growl and flick the roller at me, splattering me with pain as well.

You put the roller back in the tray and push me to the window. You push me over, forcing my hands down on the window ledge to steady myself as your ram your hard meat inside me…. Fuck it feels so fucking good.

"This is what you have wanted all the time you scheming little bastard. You want my fucking hard tool pummelling you cunt, don't you boy? Well, I'm going to fucking ruin it! I'm going to shag you like you have never been shagged before."

You place the cigarette in your mouth and the breeze blows the smoke curl around me. You hold on to my hips, ramming your cock hard, like animals fucking. I want to cry out in a mixture of pain and pleasure but the windows are open and I would have great difficulty explaining that to the neighbours.

"Fuck," I say.

"What? You're fucking loving it"

"No, my parents are parking the car."

"Fuck me. Well I'm not stopping!" you growl.

As my parents walk up the path, you put your hand over my mouth and continue fuck me. I'm breathing rapidly through my nose as panic floods my body. I could get caught and that would not go down well. Fuck… fuck, fuck, fuck! What am I going to do? Then the doorbell rings. My heart nearly fucking stops.

"He can't be in!" my dad says.

"Don't be stupid, the windows are open."

You can't resist making things difficult for me. You draw back your cock, just to the point where it will come out, then ram it back inside me hard… BAM!! I cry out in pain but thankfully it's muffled by your hand.

"Well he might be in the garden?" my dad suggest.

"I'll just call through the window and…."

"Come along woman, we are going to be late!"

As my parents walk back down the path, you remove your hand from my mouth.

"See, nothing to fucking worry about!"

"You're fucking mental," I say, looking around.

"You fucking loved it, it was a nice bit of danger. Well, I did anyway. Come on, what did you want me to do? Pull out so you could get dressed and have you parents messing things up? I don't think so! You're my fucking boy. Mine to shag anywhere I fucking like, like the cunt you are. You got that?"

"Yes."

"What?"

"YES!"

"Good. It was fucking close though. Made me even harder inside you! Can you feel it?"

"Yeah," I pant breathlessly.

"Good! Now bend over and take it like a fucking man!"

I lean back against the window seal and your arse power drives your cock inside me once more. You're fucking so hard my feet are lifting slightly off the floor.

"I'm getting close, you little bitch. You want my muck inside you?"

"Yeah… fuck yeah."

"I'm cumming… I'm fucking cumming!"

I can feel your cock pulse as you empty your hot sweet fucking cum inside me. I can feel it hitting the walls of my insides as blast after blast of spunk fills my hole. You pull out of me and I turn around, to see you panting, your cock still dripping cum.

"Next time you fancy a session, remind me to call your parents half way through. That was fucking horny."

"I don't think so!" I pant. "We should get on."

"Oh no you don't! This bad boy is still fucking hard. I'm not done with you yet!

You move the stuff so the paint doesn't get knocked over and sit on the floor, leaning against the settee.

"Don't let any of that shit drip out; I need that as fucking lube."

I straddle you and lower my fucked, cum soaked hole down onto you hard meat. You grab the remote control and switch on the football.

"Do you have to watch that now?"

"Yeah. There isn't much time left and the scores nil nil. Just fucking ride me!"

I begin to move my hole up and down your shaft again. My hand strokes your shaved head and for a moment your eye leaves the screen to glance at me, before flashing back. 'I'll get his fucking attention!' I think to myself. I ride you harder and faster, bouncing like a bucking bronco at a rodeo. You light another cigarette and exhale a large lungful of smoke, which fucking turns me on. I run my fingers over your chest, a usual guarantee to raise more than just a smile. But your eyes remain looking over my shoulder.

"Argh fuck, that feels so fucking good."

"Yeah… I know," you say, not paying any attention. "Yes," you shout, as you team scores just before the final whistle.

"Oh, you're back with me then?"

"Come on Nick, footy and a fuck...what could be better? What the fuck are you doing, put some fucking effort into it! We are not your fucking parents you know!"

You take another long drag on your cigarette, your balls still hanging out of me and stretch your arms out along the seat of the settee. Your body rocks and I fuck you harder.

"Come on Nick, put your fucking back into it. I want some fucking effort!"

I'm panting louder and my arse is raping your dick. Your shaft slices inside me, almost rearranging my internal organs. But it's still not good enough for you. You put your tattooed hand on my throat and hold it tight. You lift me with your other arm, pushing me back until there is enough room for you to lie between my legs. Your hands grip my shoulders as your arse takes over, dictating the speed and ferocity of your fucking. I put my hands on your back, knowing I'm touching your SKINHEAD tattoo across your shoulders, which turns me on even more.

"This is how you get fucked. Fucked by a hard fucking skinhead cunt!"

"Fuck...mate....you're...going ...to break...my...pelvis," I gasp.

"That's right, fucking take it. You know you're being used! I don't fucking care if I break you. I want to break you! It would remind you that you have been fucked by a real fucking skinhead Boss!"

You lift yourself up onto your hands, straightening your tattooed arms and locking them to hold your body above me.

"I'm getting close. You want my muck inside you again?"

"Yes!"

"Tell me how much you want my cum. Beg me to fill you with my fucking little skinhead bastards!"

"Fuck yeah, please fill me. I really need your cum inside me. I want to carry you inside me all fucking day. Give me your D.N.A Pitch, please... I need it... please... please...please!"

"I'm Cumming," you bellow and grit you teeth.

You ram your cock as hard as you can, as you shoot another load inside me, thrusting with every spurt. You drop down on top of me before rolling off, taking another drag from your cigarette.

"Fucking hell, I needed that," you pant.

"I... don't think... I can... move."

"Well you can stay there, I have to get my head down if we are going to this Skin night tonight," you say, wiping the sweat from your forehead on the back of your arm.

"Oh fuck. I forgot about that!"

"Close everything up and come to bed. I will expect you up there in 5 minutes. OK?"

"Sure."

Part 2

The night came soon enough. The heat from the day still lingered and as we arrived at the club, it was already filling quickly. The music was loud and the heat struck us immediately as we walked in. My eyes wandered around the groups straight skin men. We walked over to the bar and ordered our drinks.

"Oi, ignoring me, you bastard?"

I turned around to see a huge, intimidating bloke, built like a brick shit house, standing smiling at you, his head razor shaved smooth. He wore a checked, shirts and bleachers, with large 20 hole boots hugging his legs.

"Nah mate, not at all," you reply, shaking his hand and patting is shoulder. "Steve, mate… this is Nick."

"Hi," I smile.

"Alright?"

"This is his first time," you smile.

"A virgin? Well, we will have to show you a good time then, wont we mate?"

"Cheers," I manage to say, smiling before taking a nervous sip from my larger.

"He is a little shy," you grin.

"Shy? And he is hanging around with you? I would have thought you would have fucked that out of him by now mate!"

"Believe me, I'm trying!" you grin, taking a large mouthful of larger.

"Becky is around here… somewhere!"

"Is she OK? How's the kids?"

"Still breathing… just!"

***

The night passed quickly. The music played on, we talked danced and I finally began to relax. It seemed as though we had only had a couple of drinks before everyone started leaving. The heat was now stifling and most of the men were bare-chested. Steve had quite a collection of tattoos, which I have to admit… caught my attention. As things were winding up, Steve pulled you close and kissed you full on the mouth.

"See, not bad for a straight bloke!"

"Passable," you grin.

"Come on mate. Let's get outside!"

"What about your wife?" I asked naively.

"Don't worry, she can't go anywhere. We are getting a taxi and I've got the money. Come on, it should be cooler outside."

The night air was still warm but a welcome relief from the confined furnace of the club. We walked up an alley and around to the back of the club. You and Steve kiss again. Great, just what I need... a floor show! Suddenly Steve starts to undo his bleachers.

"Come on then… show me what it's like with a guy?"

I was confused. I know the old saying… what's the difference between a straight man and a gay man? 6 pints… but to witness it first-hand (and from such a massive, straight man) was slightly unnerving.

"Well you heard the man…" you bark, "…get your bleachers down!" I don't know what it was… the heat from the club or the fresh air hitting me after all that lager but I fumbled around at my jeans. "Fucks sake!" you sigh, and yank down my bleachers.

Steve pushed me over a bin, spits on his hand, which he rubs on his cock and pushes it into me hard. I shout out in a mixture of pain and pleasure.

"Oh fuck, you're right. It is different from a cunt!" Steve smiles.

"I don't know why, he is a little cunt. I take it now is not the time to tell you I fucked two loads into him earlier." you laugh.

"You dirty bastard!" Steve grins.

My body jolts with his hard thrusts. I'm not sure if he just likes it hard and rough or he is trying to make a point but I bite my lip and take it. Steve holds out his arm and you step closer. He put his hand on your back and starts to suck on your nipple as you stroke the back of his smooth shaved head.

"Fuck him Steve. Rape that fucking hole. Fuck my boy!"

You and Steve start to kiss again as I cry out in pleasure. I felt weird being fucked by someone else while you are so close. But you are OK with everything, so who am I to argue?

"Mate, I'm getting close. I'm gonna cum soon!"

"Yeah fucking breed him Steve."

Steve clasps my hips and pushes as hard as he could. He throws his head back and grits his teeth. "Fuck!" he bellows as his cock pumps his hot sticky cum inside me. I cry out and move with his trusts as his cock drains every drop into me. Panting, Steve starts to pull up his bleachers.

"Fucking hell. I can see why you're fucking him!"

"Not bad is he?" you grin.

"Right, I had better get back and see if that stupid bitch has called a taxi yet. See you both again soon."

And with that, Steve walks off back down the alley to the street.

"Are you fucking me now?" I ask.

"Nah. I'm in the mood for bit of comfort tonight. I'm going to fuck you in bed."

I pull up my jeans and we walk back to the alley with your arm draped over my shoulder.

It eventually took 6 months to paint the lounge… with all the interruptions!!!

Just to make sure

I cry out as your cock pushes deeper and deeper inside me. Your knuckles are almost turning white as you grip my skin, forcing my body back onto you. My fingers grip the spindles of the dinning chair as the leather straps binding my wrists to it began to dig in.

"Take it Nick. Fucking take it!"

"Oh God... fuck me!"

Just then there is a ring on the doorbell.

"Fuck off," you shout, your cock driving into me again and again.

The doorbell rings again and you pull out of me.

"What the... you can't answer it like that?" I say.

"Why not...scared it's your fucking parents?" you say, disappearing out of the room.

You open the door, which stops suddenly as the chain tightens.

"Who the fuck is it?" you bark. Then, the figure of man moves into view. "Steve!"

"Hello mate, you alright? I knocked next door; they told me it was this house. They gave me a funny look... half 'oh my God, it's another one' and half, like it was the most natural thing in the world."

"That's probably because I'm here a lot," you laugh. "Hang on."

You close the door and slide across the door chain, before opening it to show the world you're naked. The light from the street lamps bathed your body, showing Steve the beast is still standing to attention.

"Fucking hell mate. I bet that does some damage!"

"You will have to ask Nick. Come in mate."

"Fuck mate, I didn't know you had your weapon inked. I really needed a chat but I don't think this is the right time."

"Bollocks. We're mates! That's what mates are for."

"Rebecca has got herself fucking pregnant," he says, walking into the room, the conversation tailing off. "Fucking hell!"

"Hi Steve," I smiled

"Did I say you can talk?" you snap, before directing the conversation back to Steve. "Have you forgotten you have already fucked him?"

"No, ya bastard! It's just, I was drunk….and that was months ago."

"Well, how about you reacquaint yourself? Just to make sure you enjoyed it the first time. You get undressed and I'll carry on!"

"Ace mate. Cheers" Steve smiles.

You kneel back behind me and push back into me, grabbing my shoulder and carry on at the furious pace before you were disturbed.

"So, another kid. How many is that now?"

"4 with her. Six in total," Steve says, taking of his shirt and undoing his bleachers.

"Ya fertile cunt!" you smile, watching him undress.

My finger s gripped the spindles of the chair again and I rest my head on the wooden seat. WHAM, you slap my arse and leaves a red hand print. I cry out in pain but it cuts no ice. My mind flashes back to that night, fucking in the darkness behind the club on a night out. The scent of sweaty skinhead poured back up my nostrils, lodging itself in my throat and I had to admit, it would be good to get fucked by him again. I wanted to move my hand down between my legs and feel your balls as you fuck me. But as I try to move them, the strap cuts deeper into me. I hate being fucked from behind. I love seeing your body as you move, the ink getting brighter and more vivid as the sweat rolls down your body. Your grip on my hips tightened as your fingers dig into me.

"I'm getting close. I'm gonna fucking cum," you shout.

At that moment, Steve wraps his arms around your chest and pulls you backwards.

"No you're fucking not!" he says, as you lay panting on the carpet.

"Cunt!" you laugh. Steve wanks his cock, trying to work himself up. "You can't even get it up, you dopey bastard. That will fucking teach ya to cut a man of when he is just about to blow!"

Steve doesn't answer. He just raises his middle finger and carries on wanking. With his cock now hard Steve rams it inside me. I shout out as he starts to thrust just has hard and fast as you.

"So, how's it feel?" you laugh, laying on your back and wiping the sweat from your forehead with the back of your hand.

"Nice mate. And you've kept it warm for me."

"Memories coming flooding back?" you smile, sitting up and resting yourself on your elbows. "Go on my son!"

Steve looks rounds and laughs, raising his middle finger again as you laugh.

"You know what, I can't do it like this," Steve said, leaning across my back and struggling with the straps around my wrist.

I watched as his tattooed arms, reached around me and I can feel the stubble on his chest against my back and the metal rings through his nipples.

"Fuck, I was enjoying that!" you sigh.

"Nah mate, I like a bit more movement. Besides, I have plans for this cunt."

"With my hands now free, I rub my wrists to try and get the blood back into them. I gingerly turn round as my back is stiff from being stooped over for so long. "Don't get too comfortable, I'm putting you to work!"

It was only now I could get a good look at him in the light. His razor shaved head was smooth, the perfect complement to his classic, rugged good looks. My eyes scanned his body, the tattoo of a chain around his neck, the bulldog on his chest moving as he pants and the faint line of stubble from his pubes climbing up his rhythmically moving belly towards his belly button and beyond. As Steve leant over to his denim jacket, extending his heavily tattooed arms to get his cigarettes, I noticed the top of a sword tattoo jutting out from the top of his 25 hole boots and the flash of a devil tattoo on his arse cheek.

"Work?" I questioned.

"Riding me you stupid cunt, not cleaning or housework or shit."

"Oh right. Cool," I panted.

Steve lay on his back and I lifted my leg over him. I placed my hand down between my legs and held up his cock as I lowered my fuck hole. I slide my fingers over his shaved pubes and slowly up his belly. I leant forward, placing one hand on the carpet and the other on his chest. Steve places a cigarette in his mouth, before throwing the packet over you. Steve lights his fag and throws the light over as well. I sit up and close my eyes as I feel Steve's shaft sliding deep inside me. You light up a cigarette and you throw the packets back at him. It lands on his chest before you throw the lighter back.

"Cunt," Steve smiles, picking up the packet and lighter, before placing them on the carpet next to him.

You smile and get up on your knees, shuffling over to us as you smoke.

"Alright mate," Steve says, looking up at you.

"Lick my balls," you say.

Steve lifts himself up on his elbows and starts to run his tongue over your balls. He lifts himself up on his hands, locking his arms in place, opens his mouth and takes your cock inside. You put your head back and close your eyes, exhaling a long plume of smoke. You place your hand on his scalp, originally to push his head onto your cock but you stroke it, loving the feeling. Steve closes his eyes and gags as you push his head down your shaft.

"Sorry mate," he said, not wanting to look like a wimp.

"No worries. You haven't done it that often. But you will have to learn. I'm sure the boy can show you!"

I look up at you, then down at Steve.

"Yeah... sure." I manage to say.

"He is usually a lot more vocal than this!"

"It's OK. He is not used to having two tops to service," Steve laughs, looking up at you. He inhales a large lungful of smoke before exhaling over me.

"Fucking hell! His cunt just tightened! It almost crushed my dick!"

"I'm not surprised, he likes blokes smoking when he is getting fucked!"

"Yeah? I will remember that! Anything else?"

"Plenty mate but that can wait. Except for a nice big fucking wad inside him!"

"The way I'm going, I'll probably fucking knock him up too," Steve laughed, inhaling again and blowing the smoke over me.

"You had better not, that's my job," you laugh. "Open your mouth!"

"What?" Steve ask, concerned.

"Open… your… fucking… mouth!"

"You aren't gonna piss I it or something are ya?"

"No. Now open!"

Stephen takes another lungful of smoke and exhales, tilts his head back so he is looking at your bollocks and open his mouth. He rocks as I continue to ride his shaft as you spit into his mouth, a long trail of saliva hanging from your lip, which eventually falls into his mouth.

"Now feed it to him!" you bark.

Steve lifts his head upright, his tongue out with your spit still on it. I lean forward, my mouth open and our lips connect. Our tongues rolling and flicking as the exchange takes place. As our lips part he looks at me and smiles, before spitting in my face.

"I like that. I like that a lot."

"Good. Now get your dick out of him and let me have a go!"

I gently lift myself up and Steve's hard cock thudded against his abs. I laid down my back and spread my legs as you knelt down, your boots creaking, stirring memories of the times we have fucked in them up alleys before. You lean over me, placing one hand down on the carpet by my chest and guiding your rod in with the other. Then with a hard ram and a jolt from my body, you are in. After a couple of hard thrusts from your hips, just to reclaim your territory, you look over at Steve and smile.

"Now watch the master at work… again."

Steve sat on the settee, his legs open a little and his cock still hard and rigid, watching as he continued to smoke. You hold out your cigarette butt and hand it to him, which he stubs out in the ashtray.

"Go on mate; nail him to the fucking floor!" Steve grins.

You look back down at me, with an intensity in your eyes. It was an unnerving stare, almost daring me to have enjoyed his cock better than yours, just so you can administer punishment. I closed my eyes and gasped as your thrusting got harder and faster. When I opened my eyes, that intense stare was still burning into me. I ran my hands up your straight tattooed arms supporting your body and rub your smooth shaved scalp; that I had only shaved a couple of hours before. I can feel your cock twitch inside me and I know I had the reaction that I wanted.

"I'm gonna cum… I'm gonna fucking cum."

"Yeah go on mate, fucking flood him!" Steve egged on. "Hang on, no don't…"

But you weren't listening. You were not holding back for him or for anyone. I bend my knees and your borrowed boots rub against your arse. You jab your cock inside me as it explodes, pumping thick jets of cum deep inside me.

"Oh God," I shout in pleasure, as you pick up the up pace again.

"No... You're not going again?"

"Of course. I always do," you boast, massaging you own ego while deflating Steve's at the same time.

I keep panting and grunting as your cock keeps pounding me, lubricated with your own liquid. I arch my back and watch as the sweat drips from your face.

"Argh... take that you cunt," you growl, as your cock pumps another thick white load inside me. You thrust intermittently, making sure every last sperm is out before you look over to Steve panting.

"Your turn!"

"Oh mate, I really don't think I could get up his cunt with your spunk up there! I...."

"Just do it. Stop being some whining little pussy and fuck him."

Steve got off of the settee and changed places you. You flop down on the settee, wiping your face and panting loudly. Steve lies on top and positions his cock in place.

"Fucking get in there," you bark and push his arse down with the sole of your boot. His cock slides in full length and he gasps.

"Argh fuck, it's all fucking wet."

"You're meant to be a fucking man."

As Steve began to fuck, he started to relax. The ease with which is cock was moving made it different, nicer somehow. And once he had got his head around the fact that he was fucking your cum... he stared to enjoy it. He lowered his body down onto mine, gripped my shoulders and started to almost rape my hole.

I shouted out again and his meat skewered me. I could feel the warmth of his skin as our bodies stick together from the sweat covering me.

"You want me to top you up? You want my bastards to mix with his? Do ya boy?"

"Yes," I managed, almost whispering.

"Do ya?" he shouted?

"Yes," I shouted back.

Steve's grip intensified as he pushed his tool as deep inside me as he could. His cock spasmmed as is blasted his thick hot cum deep inside me.

"Oh my God. Oh my fucking God," he managed, and he lay panting inside me.

Silence. The only sound that could be heard was Steve's panting and he lay with his eyes closed, his hands still gripping my shoulders.

"Steve? Are you dead mate?" you ask.

Steve rolled off, onto his back and placed the back of his hand on his forehead.

"Fucking hell. That was unreal. I need a fag," he smiles, looking over at you. You take two cigarettes and light them both, keeping one for yourself and passing the other to Steve.

"Looks like you need that," you grin.

Part 2

The night is warm and we are laying on the bed, you, Steve and me lying in the middle. All with our boots still on. The duvet has been folded up and dropped on the floor at the end of the bed. You wake up and sit up with a jolt, wondering where you are. You shake me vigorously and I wake with a start.

"What? What's up?" I ask.

"Shush," you whisper. "Come with me."

***

You get up off of the bed, then I slide myself off and carefully stand up. I follow you through to the lounge and you click on the light.

"What's up?"

"Nothing, I just wanted some time with you myself. Don't get me wrong, he is a mate but he doesn't know when to fuck off. He should be back with his own fucking family!"

I grin to myself.

"Are you...Do you not want to share anymore?" I joke.

"Shut up, and suck this!" you smile.

You place your hand on my shoulder and push me down. I drop to my knees and open my lips, taking your cock into my mouth. I close my eyes and savour the taste of you. You place your hand on the back of my head, pushing my face onto you whilst rubbing my freshly shaven scalp. My head bobs backwards and forth on the meat between your legs and you close your eyes and just enjoy being taken inside my warm, wet mouth. You look over at your reflection in the mirror above the sideboard. You pose, looking at yourself, before you run your hand up your arm, watching it glide over you tattoos, before doing the same with the other arm. You run your hand over your smooth head and continue watching yourself.

"Get up. Get over there," you bark.

You push me over to the sideboard and stand behind me. Your eyes look down as you position your cock, grab my hips and slide you meat inside me.

"Oh fuck yes," you smile.

You push my body down onto the flat wooden top of the sideboard and your eyes return to the image before you. It was not your reflection looking back, it was a man… a man reclaiming what is rightfully his…a skin head man who is using his boy for his own gratification… a skinhead man who knows what he wants and is taking it at any cost. This was the man… a master… who wanted sex, and was taking it. There is only room for one alpha male in the house and that man… that skinhead man. And the man looking back at you from the mirror. Your eyes scanned your own image, the smooth skin of your shaven head, the thickness of your inked neck and the broadness of your shoulders and chest. Your eyes moved down your body and watched as your own hips moved rhythmically behind me. You deliberately ram your cock in harder and watch the expression on my face change.

"You like that boy?"

"I love it."

"I love it what?

"I love it, sir."

"That's better! You want my cum inside you again?"

"Yes sir. Give it to me!"

Your eyes fix back on your heavily tattooed arms before moving up to your face. You watch yourself as you get closer and closer.

"I'm gonna cum," you watch yourself say, "I'm gonna fucking cum, you bastard."

I open my eyes and look at you watching yourself. I tighten my arse muscles and your cock explodes inside me. Bam…thick jet of hot spunk blasts inside me. Bam… Bam…Bam. You lean forward as your cock is still pumping and bit my neck in your teeth. I try to muffle my cry so as not to wake the whole street, let alone Steve.

"What was that for?"

"Just reminding everybody who you really belong to!" you growl. "Come on, let's go back to bed."

***

After a piss, we both lay back on the bed and in your post spunking satisfaction, you are quickly asleep again. I lay in the darkness reflecting what had just happened, when Steve got up out of bed and walked through to the en-suite. In the quiet of the night, he sounded loud as he pissed in the water of the toilet bowl before flushing.

"Nick… Nick?"

"What?"

"Good, you're awake. Come through here," he whispered.

***

I got out of bed and followed Steve through to the lounge, clicking on the light and dimming the switch.

"What?" I ask.

"I just wanted to say, I have really fucking enjoyed myself tonight."

"I don't mean to be rude mate but it three o'clock in the morning. Can't this wait?"

"No. Because he will be awake in the morning. Plus, I want a fuck now!"

Steve grabbed the back of my head and pulled me towards him. Our lips touched and before long, I was stroking his smooth shaven head. My other hand wandered down to this nipple and I began to play. Our lips broke and he looked at me, smiling.

"Fucking hell, that's so good. You have done things tonight that Becky doesn't even know exists."

"And you like?"

"I like a lot."

"You want me to suck you?" I whisper.

"No. I just wanna be inside you again. Now, lay on your back." I lay down and Steve kneels in front of me. "Spread your legs, bitch."

"I bet you say to all the girls!"

"Yeah. And it works. Now, let me in!"

Steve's forehead touches mine and I can feel the warmth of this breath on my skin. He pushes and gasps under his breath as his cock inches in, until I can feel his balls touching me. This wasn't the fast fucking from before, nor was it the gentle love making you see in the movies. It was kind of in between.

"You like the feel of me inside you?"

"Fuck yeah."

"Of course you do. You like real men. Proper fucking skins. I watched you in that club all those months ago… you were like a kid in a candy shop."

"You blame me?" I smiled.

"No. because at the end of the night, you still managed to get fucked by the two best looking blokes in the place! Even with my bird there. That was a fucking turn on, I can tell ya."

"You're telling me," I grinned.

All of a sudden, a pair of boots stand next to us. Steve looks up and sees you looking down at him. Steve straightens his arms and smiles an embarrassed smile.

"Sorry mate. I woke up and had an itch that needed scratching."

"Don't worry about it." you say calmly. "I have already got my own back!"

"What? How?" Steve asks, stopping in mid stroke.

"I came in him about twenty minutes ago," you laugh.

"You bastard," Steve smiles, not sure if he should believe you. "Did he?"

"Yep, I smile.

"Oh well, in for a penny."

Steve starts fucking again. He picks up the pace, half to enjoy himself and half to show off in front of you….as if!

"Go on ya fucker, your meant to be fucking him, not fucking dancing. Screw him for fucks sake!" you growl.

Steve is now fucking as though his life is depending on it. His tattooed arse cheek is pushing his cock so deep inside me, it feel like his knob is going to come out of my mouth. His cock spurts another big load inside me, his shaft twitching as it empties the prize inside me.

As Steve rolls off, you look at the clock.

"Quarter to four… not much point in going back to bed now. Might as well have a beer and keep fucking," you smile.

For the future

Its Saturday afternoon, the sun is high in the sky and the warm breeze is blowing through the open window. We are sitting on the settee, you are just in your boxers and I just have a t-shirt on. Your tattooed arm is over my shoulder and your fingers are playing with my nipple as we watch the TV.

Suddenly, there is a knock on the door.

"Who the fuck is that?"

"I don't know. I'm not expecting anyone." I advise. "I will try and get rid of them."

I walk through the hall and open the door slightly. Steve was standing before me in a white sleeveless vest, bleachers and long black boots.

"Alright. Is Pitch here?"

"Steve! Yeah, but…"

"Good. I haven't seen him for months," he said, pushing past me and walking through to the lounge.

"Come in," I say to myself and close the door.

"Steve!"

"Hello mate. Not seen you for ages."

"No... you know what it's like. Just been working and shagging. As you do!"

"Yeah mate, I know what you mean," you chuckled.

"I just wanted to show you something. My mate got me this new camcorder, its fucking brilliant. I have just been to my boys school sports day. Got it all on here."

"Kids school sports day?" you say, deep in thought.

"Yeah. I came third in the father's race. Well, it's hard to run in fucking boots isn't it? Anyway, I beat that cunt Mark Hodges, that's all I'm worried about.

"I have an idea… back in a minute."

Steve sits down on the armchair and I take my seat back on the settee.

"I'm sorry, where's my manners? Do you want a drink?"

"Sure. Lager would be nice."

I walk out to the kitchen and open the fridge door. I take out three cans of lager and kick the door closed. I return to the lounge, hand Steve his can and return to the settee. Steve placed the camera on the floor, opened the can and takes a large mouthful.

"Are you hot boy?" he growled.

"Yeah."

"I thought so. Sitting like that I can see your cunt. Brings back memories of me slamming my cock inside you. Does that turn your on boy?" he asked, taking another drink form his can.

"Yeah," I say, my eyes flashing to the door.

Steve stood up and walked over, dropping down next to me. He placed his can down on the floor and reaches over, running his middle finger around my hole. He inserted the tip and made a circular motion, before pushing it in. I gasped, trying to play it cool… and failing miserably.

"You like me in your cunt again boy?"

"Yes," I managed to whisper.

"Well, if you're a good boy…and your Boss is in a good mood, you might get more than just a fucking finger!"

"Steve? Turn that camera on!"

"Hang on," Steve shouts, pulling his finger from my cavity and reaching over to get the cam. "It's on," he said, pointing it at the door.

You came in, stark bollock naked; your arms held out like the crucified skinhead, your large black boots hugging your legs.

"My name is Pitch and welcome to my… Fuckumentary!" you manage to say, before laughing.

Steve burst out laughing and I watch, smiling to myself.

"You are a fucking legend," Steve laughs, still holding the camera at you.

"I am going to fuck him… him! Steve, turn the fucking camera round!" Steve spins the camera round to me, before moving it back onto you. "And if he ends up getting knocked up," you continue, "… this is where you came from… my fucking balls and my tattooed cock," you saying, breaking off into laughter.

"You're fucking mental," Steve laughs.

"What?" you smile. "I have to show my little cunt where he came from...before I show him how he was made!"

"You…" you say, pointing to me, "… take the fucking camera. And you…" you say, pointing to Steve, "… get fucking undressed."

I take the camera and Steve eagerly starts to undress. I put the camera on Steve as he pulls his vest over his head and drops it onto the settee. He puts up his middle finger, smiling broadly as he starts to unbuckle his bleachers.

I put the camera back onto Pitch. You light a cigarette and throw the packet over to Steve.

"You probably won't see this until you're about eighteen, so this is how I look when I fucking made ya." Steve laughed off camera. "Start at the top… nicely shaved head, essential. Moving down, broad fucking chest and if I turn around, skinheads across my shoulders. If I turn back to the front and he moves the camera down a bit further, my ink. You will probably notice that I haven't got as much as I have when you're watching this, that's because I'm always adding. But this is me today.

Then moving down to the business end, my fucking packet. Look at that boy, nice pair of full bollocks and your old mans inked knob and shaft. Then, the boots… always fucking in me boots... and you should be too. Are you fucking ready yet?" Steve comes into shot and stands next to you, also naked with his boots on. He stands next to you and you put your arm over his shoulder. "And this fucker is my old mate Steve. Your Uncle Steve. He's straight but then no-bodies perfect… except me!"

"Alright?" Steve chuckles. "At the time this is being made, I already have six kids. So if cunt-boy over there does end up pregnant, you're probably my bastard anyway," Steve laughed.

"Fuck off. If you have a court order by the time you're ten… I'm your father," you grin.

"And if you have a kid of your own, by the time your twelve… I'm your father," Steve laughed.

You smile and push him away from you, jokingly.

"OK boy, get down here!" you bark.

Steve takes the camera and I kneel down in front of you, your cock already half erect from messing about.

"Lesson one… daddy gets his cock sucked!" I open my mouth and take your knob inside. "OK, the swallow is in… now for the shaft!" I slide my lips down your meat to about half way. The camera flashes from my mouth to your face. "Half way there… watch the letters disappear." My lips engulf the rest of your meat. The camera moves back up to your face. "There, all gone… my tool is down his throat and his face is in my pubes. See my balls hanging out of his mouth?" you say, taking another large drag on your fag.

The camera comes back onto me as I slide my head backwards and forwards on your dick. Then Steve moves back and sits on the settee, getting a full length shot of you standing getting pleasured. Your hand comes up from your side and pushes on the back of my head as you continue to smoke.

Steve pulls the coffee table over and places the camera on top. He stands up and the camera watches his tattooed arse as he walks over to you. He opens a can of lager and hands it to you, as he takes a sip of his own and continues to smoke. You take a mouthful and swallow, before you and Steve kiss. You give the camera the middle finger before your hand slides down his back and onto his arse. The camera picks up the sound of your lips smacking and your hand rubbing and grabbing his arse cheek with the tattoo of a devil on it. You move your finger to his arse hole and he laughs and pulls away from you.

"Nah Pitch, I'm not fucking ready for that."

"Fair enough," you say, looking at him as you continue to move your hips.

I was concentrating on the job in hand, savouring the taste of you as my mind wondered. I had never been filmed before and this was a turn on. Plus, the joking commentary of talking to a potential son was also having the desired effect.

"Right, moment of truth," you say, pulling out of my mouth. I stand up and you lay on the floor, side on to the camera. I straddle you and lower myself down onto your solid tool. I cry out as your cock slices into me. "Shut up and take it! Is that camera positioned right?"

Steve walks over and checks the display.

"Yeah. Everythings fine!"

I start to ride you and again you give the camera the finger. I look down and watch as you move beneath me as my cunt moves up and down your dick. You look up at me and smile, as you keep glancing over at the camera.

"I hope you're enjoying my fuckumentory, boy? Watching your father fucking!"

"No, your father will be fucking shortly son," Steve laughs, off camera.

"You're such a fucking prick," you smile. "Steve, pass me the camera here."

Steve picks up the camera and hands it to you. You steady it and hold it just above your chest.

"Nick, lift up your balls." I lift up my balls and you get a clear shot. "Fuck... look at the tattooed fucker working. That's not only going to make a baby but a fucking football team by the time I'm finished. Fuck, I love watching the letters disappear and reappear." You hold the camera at arms length and position it back on your face. "When you're fucking old enough, I will take you to get your first piece of ink but it probably won't be your manhood. Take this," you say and Steve grabs the camera.

He runs the camera around behind us and watches as my hole continues going up and down your shaft.

"Fuck," I say.

"Take it you fucking little cunt. I'm gonna breed you."

As the camera comes back around to the side of us, I stroke your head before sitting back upright. You gob on my chest and pant as the fucking continues.

"OK, change of position," you grin.

You roll me over and lay between my legs. The camera watches as your arse starts pounding between my legs.

"Fucking take it," you growl, as I cry out. "You want me to breed your hole boy?" you say, looking down at me. "You want me to fucking breed you?" You look up, into the camera that Steve is still holding. "Yeah take this skinhead meat… take my fucking meat as you get fucked by a skinhead man. Fucking carry me around inside you, ya bitch!" You look down at me. You have that intense stare, the look that is only focusing on one thing… getting yourself off. "I'm getting close. When I cum, you will have my fucking little cunt inside you." You stare back into the camera, your eyes almost burning. "I'm cumming… I'm fucking cumming," you shout, ramming you cock inside me as deep as you can as your cock blasts jets of thick white cum inside me. You lay motionless, your body jolting every now and then as your cock dispenses the last of your sperm. "In fucking nine months, he will be pushing my boy out of his cunt," you pant, looking into the camera.

"Bollocks!" Steve says, placing the camera back down on the coffee table, and standing up. "Shift, ya arse… I'll show ya how to fucking do it." I go to get up but Steve places his boot sole on my chest "Where are you going, bitch? You're fucking stay there. I'll show you how you really fuck!" Steve lies on me, fumbling to get his hard cock in position before pushing into me hard. "Now, watch a master shagger at work," he says, looking into the camera. Pitch stands up, light a cigarette and walks through to the kitchen, as Steve carries on. "It takes a real man to fuck a cunt with another bloke's cum in it!" he continues, "… I'm young, fit, fertile and a skinhead. Of course this bastard will be mine. As I said before, I already have six kids. But I will still be back to fuck him while he is swollen and I have taken over his body. I may even get a text when he is squeezing you out," he grinned. Steve stopped thrusting. "Pitch?"

"What?" you called.

"Can I ask a favour mate? Could you bring me another beer?" You come through with the cold can, and drop Steve's cigarettes and lighter next to him. "Cheers mate."

Steve opens the can and takes several gulps of cool refreshing lager. I looked up at him, supported on is straight arm. His tattoos of a chain coming around his neck, the bulldog on his chest and the large designs on his arms stood out against his slightly tanned skin.

"Steve, I….."

"Shut up! Just lay there and enjoy me inside you!" he barked, looking back down at me. He placed the can down on the coffee table, making the camera wobble a little, before lighting his cigarette, inhaling deeply and taking it out. "Here Pitch, pick up the camera and film my arse fucking." You take another drag of your cigarette, pick up the camera and stand astride his feet. Steve starts fucking again and grunting for the camera. From where you are standing, you watch as his arse pounds up and down, his cheeks tightening and releasing as he works. Steve looks over his shoulder, "Can you see it mate?"

"Yep," you reply.

"Fucking nice one. OK mate, you can put it back down now if you like… I'm starting to get close." Pitch places the camera back down on the coffee table and sits back on the settee, sipping from your can and smoking. Steve started to fuck harder and more brutal, showing off to the camera how hard he could fuck… like he was raping some slag he had picked up on a night out. "You want my spunk? You want my seed inside you boy?"

"Yes, fuck yes."

"Here it fucking comes, cunt!"

Steve puts his head back, grits his teeth, arches his back and pushes his cock as deep inside me as he can... wham…. Wham…. Wham he thrusts, as his cock pumps his thick white mess, coating my insides. The sweat is dripping of both our bodies and he drops down on top of me panting, in what is quickly turning into a trademark.

Part 2

Steve takes another drag of his cigarette, looking over to you.

"So what's happening now?" he panted. "Are we going for round two, just to make sure?"

"Too fucking right! I've never stopped at one shag in my life and don't intend starting now! As soon as you get your dick out of him!"

"Sorry mate," Steve grins. You take a drag of your cigarette as Steve stands up, picks up the camera and pulls me up. "Have to help up the poor fucker. He is weighed down with all that cum," he laughs.

You grab my arm and lead me over to the sideboard… I knew that would be next. You push me over and ease your cock inside me, looking at yourself in the mirror. "Tighten your cunt! Don't let any cum out!" I rest my head on the back of my hands as the edge of the sideboard digs into my belly. You stand, holding onto my hips and watching yourself fucking, your cock gliding in and out easily with every movement. You move your arms and admire your artwork.

"I have always admired your ink mate," Steve is heard, off camera.

"Thanks. They do get me a lot of attention."

As Steve pans around the back of you, you catch sight of him in the mirror. Knowing that a straight man is not only with you, and you are both naked but is also filming you on the job, is making your cock even harder inside me. You pull me up; holding my face under my jaw.

"You like my boy don't you Steve?"

"Yes mate."

"He is good to use isn't he?"

"Yes mate."

"Even if his belly is fucking swollen and heavy", you smile, running your hand in circles over my belly.

"Whose ever it is mate, Steve laughs."

"I know he wants nothing more than to be carrying my little cunt, don't ya boy?"

I say nothing. Steve presses a button on the camera and it zooms in on your arse cheeks. Steve watches, almost hypnotised by the rhythmic motion. You hold out your hand and Steve puts the camera down and steps forward. You kiss and your hand drops from my jaw and cups his arse cheek. Steve puts his hand on your shoulder as your tongues dance inside each other's mouths. Steve's other hand comes around me; still standing pressed against your body and also rubs my belly. But soon, you begin to pick up the pace.

"Oh fuck, I'm getting close mate," you say as your lips part.

"Yeah? Go on my son. Fucking cum again."

"I'm going to mate."

"Fucking breed his cunt again, you sexy bastard."

Both of your hands return to my hips as you drive your hard on inside me.

"I'm gonna cum... I'm gonna fucking cum."

I cry out as your cock orgasms inside me, your legs almost shaking as you release another gallon of cum inside me.

"You bastard! you sexy fucking bastard," Steve grins.

You kiss him again and your hand rubs his smooth shaven head.

"Your fucking turn!"

Steve grabs my arm and starts to pull me to follow him.

"Come on bitch. And make sure you don't drop any!"

Steve sits down on the settee and I straddle him. Then, once in position, I slide down his hard thick pole. I ride him, a mixture of pain and pleasure etched on my face. Steve takes another long drag on his cigarette and blows out the smoke.

"I have been thinking. Once you have chucked your muck, we could piss off to the pub for a couple of hours," you say off camera.

"Yeah? I'm well up for that," Steve smiles. "I will need to get some dosh from the cash point, didn't need any for the sports day. I will have to phone the missus." You reach into his jeans, take out his mobile and pass it to him. He clicks on his mobile and places it to his ear. "You… shut the fuck up," he tells me. "Alright gal? Yeah, I'm still at Pitch's mates. I just wanted to let you know that I will be late home, so don't bother getting me dinner, I will get something 'ere. What? Well you take the fucking kids. Look Beck, I'm sure you can cope for one fucking afternoon," he says, clicking of the phone.

"Problems?" you ask.

"Moody cow! The sooner she opens her legs and has that kid the fucking better!" Steve points to the camera. "Don't you have anything to fucking do with birds mate… they're bitches, the fucking lot of them!"

There was a slight pause.

" Mate?... beer!" you reminded.

"I know, I know…. but he has to get me off first."

"For fucks sake…use your imagination!"

"What do you mean?"

"Well, once you finish this time, he will have four loads inside him. All those fucking skinhead sperm swimming around inside him… and no one in the pub will know!"

"Yeah, I see what you mean."

"And if he was knocked up, what's better than boasting that we did that. Until we get a DNA test."

"Yeah... fucking awesome. I loved boasting about all my brats."

"You finish off and we will go to the pub. It's too fucking hot to wear a t-shirt… just have braces over our bare shoulders. Have the tats on display."

"Oh yes mate. Fuck yes."

I took that as a cue and picked up the pace. His cock was even more rigid inside me than the first time we fucked at the back of the club. Steve took a large lungful of smoke and blew it out.

"I'm gonna cum," he bellowed, his mind racing with pictures you had just installed in his head.

His cock pulsed as it erupted his mess inside me, mixing with all the others.

"Stay there for just one moment!" Pitch says.

"What?" Steve asked, looking round. Come on mate, the beer is calling."

You slide open the drawer of the sideboard, take out a butt plug and throw it over to Steve, who catches with both hands.

"Stick that in him. That will make sure nothing comes out," you say, before going upstairs for a shower.